EPICENTER

BASIL JACKSON

EPICENTER

W · W · NORTON & COMPANY · INC ·

 NEW YORK

To my father,
who showed me that ideas run
the world,
and to the memory of my mother,
who taught me the patience
necessary to convert ideas into
tangible things such as this book

AUTHOR'S NOTE

This book is a work of fiction. All the characters are imaginary and any resemblance to any person, alive or dead, is coincidental.

In a work of this nature, where reality and imagination merge, it is impossible not to mention government agencies and organizations that actually exist, for example, the Emergency Measures Organization, the United States Atomic Energy Commission, Atomic Energy of Canada Limited, the Atomic Energy Control Board, the Canadian Nuclear Association, and the Dominion Observatory.

The operation of a complex and highly sophisticated center such as a nuclear power station is automated. Each reactor and its associated equipment and controls combine a technology embracing nuclear physics, chemistry, electronics, and electrical and mechanical engineering, all closely interrelated. But the station inevitably has to rely on trained human beings to set the controls in operation and interpret the signals from the instruments. I have simplified the description of the operational procedures and station structure to avoid describing complicated processes.

Could such a catastrophe happen in real life? With the elaborate safety precautions built into nuclear stations the chances of disaster are remote, although less serious accidents have already occurred in some stations. That the possibility exists is recognized,

AUTHOR'S NOTE

and this alarms some people, especially as they see the proliferation of nuclear power stations across America, many of them near cities. Sixteen stations are already operating in the United States, and eighty-four more are on order, with fourteen others on the drawing boards. Many are multireactor stations. In Canada two stations are operating and three are under construction. Britain has thirteen operating, and more have been ordered. France has nine working, and others are operating in Russia, West and East Germany, Japan, Switzerland—one narrowly escaping damage from the crash of a sabotaged airliner—Italy, Spain, Sweden, India, and Holland. Nuclear stations have been ordered or are being planned by Pakistan, Bulgaria, Czechoslovakia, Hungary, Argentina, Belgium, Austria, Greece, Finland, Taiwan, Korea, Rumania, Australia, and Mexico.

By the year 2000 there will be more than five thousand nuclear reactors operating in the world, the vast majority of them in nuclear electric generating stations.

In my story I have fictionalized a regional director of the Emergency Measures Organization as a man lacking confidence. Since there are only a few officials holding such positions, I extend any apologies that may be necessary to all EMO officers. They are most efficient and, due to their rigorous training, confident and able men.

Basil Jackson

EPICENTER

ONE

The night was clear, with a cold easterly wind that stung Raymond Johnson's face. It was a good-looking, rugged face, now creased in thought, with a sharp nose and gray eyes overshadowed by shaggy eyebrows. He'd wound a plain brown scarf twice around his neck, and the front of it covered a squared-off chin and full mouth. He wore a heavy topcoat with an old-fashioned cut, not quite the style a thirty-five-year-old man with modern tastes would wear.

He had a lot to think about as he strode along the snow-covered path of the island. He wondered about the price of furniture, and how long it would take to spread fresh paint on the walls of the small bachelor apartment in the east end. It had been four years since he'd gone out to buy a bedroom suite and other furniture. Now he would have to go through it all again, but this time for himself. At least he'd be able to furnish it the way he wanted, instead of having to live with those hideous period pieces Rita had insisted on buying.

At the thought of Rita the creases around his mouth and nose deepened. He imagined her lying on the sun-baked beach in Barbados, her bikini-clad body the center of attention for every male within a hundred yards. She hadn't lost any time since they'd decided to separate. She'd caught the first available Sun-Worshipers' flight to the islands for a week's jaunt before worrying about her own furnishing problems in her new apartment. While he felt a heavy weight inside, Johnson also had a curious sense of relief now that the marriage was over. There was a finality about the end of the disagreements, the violent quarrels, the absolute lack of common ground, and now there was at least the hope of running his own life on more stable lines.

He came to the end of the path and took the road that would bring him to the landing. A ferry boat was approaching the dock, churning the frigid water and chunks of broken ice into white foam as the propellers reversed. He pulled back his glove and looked at his watch. Eleven fifteen. He grunted. There was plenty of time before taking over the midnight shift.

The ferry was almost empty. He stood on deck, a tall, spare figure with flapping coattails leaning against the rail. The few passengers were huddled in the drafty cabin staring blankly through the dirty windows. They were on their way home from visiting friends on the archipelago a half mile off the Toronto lakeshore or were returning from an evening of drinking and yarning in one of the yacht clubs.

Johnson pulled the scarf tighter around his neck and turned to watch the lights of the city as they dipped with the rolling of the tubby ship. Ahead lay the towering office buildings of the downtown district, with fluorescent-lit windows that glittered in the frosty night and red and green neon signs that reflected in the calmer water near the docks. The throb of the engine slackened beneath his feet, and the ferry slowed, gliding silently toward the pier. The wind fell as the vessel came into the lee of some warehouses, and he suddenly got

EPICENTER

a whiff of the city, the aroma of freshly made bread from a bakery, the stink of a diesel truck pulling on to a pier, and the mysterious smell from a chandler's store, waxy and ropy.

The ferry nosed into the dock and the bow thumped against the ancient truck tires that served as fenders. He heard chains rattle and the forward ramp crash on the dockside, and the coarse voice of one of the crew warning passengers to watch their step. He walked down the ramp and through the gate and crossed the road to his car parked near the Harbor Commissioners' Building. It started first time, despite the biting cold. He let it run until the heater warmed up, then switched on the radio and drove east, parallel to the Lake Ontario shoreline. Some light snow had fallen earlier, and the salting trucks had been out. Hard globules of rock salt pinged under the fenders as he turned on to Highway 401 and speeded up.

About twenty miles east of the downtown section Johnson turned off the highway and drove down a road that came out near a new housing development. Where the houses ended he took a tree-lined road that swept up to the main gates of what appeared to be a modern factory building. Through a gap he could see the nearby blackness of the lake. A high chain link fence surrounded the buildings, and a sign on the side of the gatehouse announced Fairfield Nuclear Power Station. The gray-headed uniformed guard, not wanting to let in the cold air by opening the window, peered through the glass, with a hand to his forehead to shut out the reflected light. He recognized Johnson and saluted.

Johnson drove through the open gate and parked near the door of the administration building where a partly snow-covered sign read R. H. Johnson, Executive Chief Engineer. He switched off, opened the door, and stamped his feet on the freshly plowed ground.

13

EPICENTER

Inside his office he hung the topcoat in a closet, put on a fresh white smock, and checked that the radiation-exposure badge was pinned to the lapel. A quick glance at his desk showed that no new mail had appeared in the In tray. He walked the remaining steps to the swinging doors of the control room.

As he entered the brilliantly lit room a short, wide-set man looked up from the console that stood before an array of instruments on the wall. He had light brown quick-moving eyes set in an open freckled face. The ends of his lips curled up momentarily in a reserved smile.

"Evening, sir," he said quietly, and turned to watch an instrument.

"All set, Charlie?"

Charles Townsend, Chief Chemical Engineer, nodded without taking his eyes from the dial. An alert man in his early thirties, with fair, almost red, hair neatly combed in a backward sweep, he used words sparingly. He exuded an aura of knowledge and authority, and when he was left in charge of the control room he dominated it with an air of one filled with supreme self-confidence. Operators on duty seemed to sense, rather than see, his presence. Like Johnson, he ruled firmly and fairly, and would stand for no slipshod operating methods or short cuts. Off duty he spent much of his time assembling do-it-yourself hi-fi kits, and a copy of the latest catalogue of new kits lay at that moment on the desk in his office next to Johnson's, under the current issue of *Atomic News Magazine*.

Johnson stationed himself behind the large desk in the center of the spacious control room and ran his eyes over the rows of instruments. He checked the number of operators on duty. Townsend peered upward, trying to read a dial high up on the wall, the back of his head turned toward Johnson.

EPICENTER

He'd never noticed that bald spot on Charlie's head before—funny how the light bounced off it and highlighted the center of the crown of hair; it made him look like an old friar. Townsend was jotting down some mysterious hieroglyphics meant only for the eyes of a select inner circle.

Johnson saw Townsend nod his head with satisfaction as he looked at the figures, then added another with that peculiar whirling motion of his ballpoint. As Executive Chief Engineer it would be Johnson's job in a few minutes to check those figures and decide if everything was ready for refueling to commence.

The refueling of the nuclear reactor was done by remote control. Once the chain reaction had begun, it was impossible for anyone to enter the sealed chamber housing the reactor because of the deadly radioactive atmosphere.

A machine was used, understandably called a refueling machine, which looked like an artillery gun. It was pointed at one of the many tubes that comprised the reactor, and a fuel bundle—a metal capsule as long as a man's arm and filled with processed uranium—was slowly pressed into the tube.

Old bundles that had been used up but were still highly dangerous were pushed out of the other end of the tube by the new ones being pressed in. They were handled by another machine and tipped into the mouth of a steel-lined chute encased in thick concrete to contain the radioactive rays.

The bundles slid down the chute to a water tank in the foundation of the station, their radioactivity smothered by the water. To make absolutely sure that the bundles ended up uncracked in the tank, a remote optical system allowed a technician to look through a glass and see inside the tank.

Johnson and Townsend peered at two closed-circuit television screens on the console. Johnson turned the knobs until the pictures of the refueling machines inside the reactor chamber came up bright and sharp. The left-hand screen showed the refueling machine charged with the fresh fuel bundles; that on the right showed the off-loading machine.

Satisfied that the pictures on the screens were as sharp as he could get them, Johnson quickly stepped to the computer console where Townsend had already stationed himself. He looked down the column of figures Townsend handed him and checked the readings. Everything appeared correct. He double-checked, and then went through the columns again.

"I'll phone MacGregor," he said, picking up the phone on the console.

"Jock, we're ready here. Call me as soon as you see the first two bundles in the tank. Is Witzensky with you?"

He heard service technician MacGregor's gruff voice, heavily overlaid with its Scottish burr, reassure him he'd inspect the bundles and that his assistant, Witzensky, was standing by.

Johnson replaced the instrument. "Commence refueling," he commanded in a quiet voice.

Townsend pressed a button on the computer console. Instantly the panel lights flashed a pattern of figures. The computer printout chattered, and Johnson leaned over Townsend's shoulder to read the signal. The computer code language announced that refueling had begun.

Everyone stared at the left-hand screen. The gunlike refueling machine started to slide across the face of the huge honeycomb of tubes in front of the reactor. Inexorably the muzzle of the gun rose to the tube to be refueled and stopped.

Johnson peered at the screen. He watched the mechanism unscrew the end cap of the tube, and imagined the deadly radioactive rays shooting out of the reactor, safely contained within the heavy-concrete domed building. Two fuel bundles were pressed into the tube. Slowly the machine screwed back the end cap.

The heads of those in the control room swiveled to the right-hand screen. The waste fuel bundles came out of the tube. The machine grabbed them. Deliberately they tipped into the mouth of the chute. Levers silently articulated. An electric motor whirled soundlessly deep inside the radioactive atmosphere and the bundles dropped out of sight down the chute.

The printout at Johnson's elbow clacked and stopped. He looked down, his eyes intent. The message reported that the first stage of refueling had been completed.

He watched the machine on the screen return to its neutral position. Before the next phase began MacGregor would check the water tank through his optical system to make sure the waste bundles had appeared in the water tank.

The atmosphere in the control room relaxed. Johnson raised his eyes to scan the instruments on the wall, and as he did so he felt a movement under his feet. An empty paper cup someone had perched near the edge of the console—unnoticed by Townsend—tipped and fell to the floor. He caught a glimpse of the television screens. The refueling machines seemed to slip out of focus. Suddenly the alarm klaxon high above the bank of dials burst into life with a deafening howl and crimson danger lights flashed across the top of the computer console.

"Check the leak detectors and the power output!" Johnson roared.

"All okay," Townsend yelled. He rushed to the klaxon control switch and flicked it off.

"It felt like a building settlement or an earth tremor," Johnson said loudly, his voice under control. He shook his head, the tiny folds of skin around his mouth quivering. He hadn't believed anything could shake the building. The station was on a foundation that rested on piles driven to bedrock, immovable legs of steel hammered into hard rock under tremendous pressure.

The telephone on the desk rang shrilly. Johnson grabbed it. His face slowly drained of color as MacGregor's voice piped out of the instrument in a thin stream. Everyone near Johnson heard it.

"The bundles 'aven't come through to the tank, sir. It felt like a vibration in the reactor building. It sorta shook, sir. I think they must 'ave got jammed somewhere in the chute!"

TWO

Alice MacGregor ran her household with Scottish thoroughness. The inside of the trim bungalow two miles from the Fairfield power station was a model of organized perfection. Because she felt that a television set in the living room upset family life, she had insisted that her husband put it in the recreation room in the basement. Jock had finished the basement himself, helped by his sixteen-year-old son Andy, and advised on the décor by Pamela, his twenty-two-year-old daughter, who at that moment was in her bedroom revising the list of things she had to do before her wedding to Ken Bates three weeks from now.

"Hey, Mom, come an' see this guy on TV!" Andy yelled up the basement steps to his mother. "He's explaining about the earthquake last night."

"Oh, Andy! I've got my hands full of baking right now. I'll be down later," Alice MacGregor called back.

Andy sat before the television set, his leg hooked over the side of the armchair that had been demoted from the living room when the MacGregors had bought a new chesterfield and armchair for the front room.

EPICENTER

His bright features reflected the bluey light from the television screen on which the face of Dr. Watson A. Gardner appeared. Gardner, a leading seismologist, was being interviewed by Maurice Telford, science columnist, journalist, and well-known television interviewer.

"Not many people know that Canada is prone to earthquakes," Gardner was saying. "We've had tremendous shocks in the past fifty years, more severe than the earthquake that destroyed Agadir, in North Africa, a few years ago and killed more than twelve thousand people. Some have been as bad as the more recent Alaska quake."

"I'm sure very few of us knew that," Telford said encouragingly.

"There have been at least a thousand earthquakes recorded in eastern Canada in the past four hundred years, and another thousand in western Canada."

"If we've had so many earthquakes, why haven't we noticed them? And why didn't they kill people?"

"Most of our more serious quakes have occurred away from populated urban areas. We've been lucky. How long our luck will hold nobody knows. Most of them have occurred deep down and their effect at the surface has been nothing more than a slight tremor."

Andy watched as the seismologist rose and walked to a large map of Canada.

"Many people believe that Vancouver on the west coast here is the only Canadian city exposed to earthquakes, because it's near California and they remember the big San Francisco quake years ago," Gardner said, pointing to a spot on the Pacific coast on the map. "But eastern Canada is just as susceptible." He paused and looked directly into the camera. A funny tingling feeling went up and down Andy's spine as he looked into Gardner's eyes.

EPICENTER

"Montreal and Quebec City are especially susceptible to earthquakes," the professor said gravely.

"What's the worst earthquake that's ever hit Canada?"

Andy took his eyes off the screen for a second to call his mother again. "Mom! You should come an' see this guy!"

"In a minute, Andy. Wait till I get this cake in the oven."

Andy watched Gardner sit in the studio chair. The seismologist's face came up big as the camera zoomed in close.

"In 1944 an earthquake almost as big as the Agadir quake hit Cornwall in eastern Ontario and Massena in upper New York State. Nobody was killed, but there was more than two million dollars' worth of damage in those two cities. That's about the worst as far as physical damage is concerned."

"What sort of damage?" Telford insisted.

"Chimneys fell and damaged roofs. A few small buildings went out of kilter. Windows broke, paving stones and some concrete sidewalks cracked. Electric power lines snapped and some sections of town had no electricity."

He smiled faintly into the cameras. Although it was his first experience on television, he was at ease. He knew his topic thoroughly and was enthusiastic and unself-conscious when he talked about it.

"Dr. Gardner," Telford said, "can you explain why so many people were killed in Agadir and nobody was in Cornwall and Massena?"

Gardner settled himself into the armchair, passed his fingertips over his forehead to wipe away a trickle of sweat caused by the heat from the studio lamps—something the studio technician had asked him not to do—and turned to Telford.

"Most of the Agadir houses were built stone on stone, and the hotels and public buildings were constructed of concrete slabs that simply collapsed. Most large public buildings and big structures in North America are steel-reinforced. Architects know we're not safe from earthquakes, as everyone once supposed. They design buildings to resist earthquakes. The tall fifty-story buildings right here in Toronto, for example, are designed to withstand earthquakes." His face broke into a smile of reassurance, and Andy relaxed, his leg still sprawled over the arm of the chair.

"How did last night's quake compare with the Cornwall and other tremors?" Telford asked, smiling warmly at Gardner.

Gardner took a battered pipe from his pocket and filled it from a plastic pouch. He was beginning to enjoy the informal atmosphere Telford created, and the way he led the conversation along to allow him to tell his story in a logical sequence. He'd been hesitant about accepting the invitation to appear on television, secretly having a slight contempt for newspapermen and the press. "They always misquote me and get the facts wrong," he once told an audience of engineers at a New York conference, and added: "You know what I mean," and reveled in the hum of approval that murmured through the hall.

"I think we could call last night's quake a serious tremor. It was nearly as powerful as the Cornwall quake," he said between puffs on his pipe.

Andy's mother joined him in the recreation room. She silently pushed his leg off the arm of the chair and looked at him sternly. Then she settled herself in the other armchair, carefully smoothed her apron, and looked at the picture on the screen.

"Would you tell us how the Dominion Observatory in Ottawa records earthquakes, Dr. Gardner?" Telford asked.

Gardner smiled and took another draw on his pipe. "The Dominion Observatory isn't the only place where we record earthquakes in Canada," he said, with a hint of condescension in his voice. "There are more than twenty stations coast to coast. Some are better equipped than others, of course, and we get reports from all of them. They use special equipment, which I'll explain in a minute."

Andy MacGregor exclaimed: "This guy's terrific!"

"What about the aftershocks of an earthquake? I understand they can be as serious as the original quake," Telford said.

"That's right. You've read about them, I'm sure. People in a serious earthquake run to the open fields and then venture back to their wrecked homes. Quite often an aftershock comes along and what remains of the shattered buildings falls on them, and there are more casualties."

"There wasn't an aftershock to last night's quake, was there?"

"No—as far as our instruments show, there hasn't been an aftershock. But then, there's still time." He smiled slyly. "We could experience an aftershock right now, right here in the studio," he added with a dramatic gesture of his arm.

Alice MacGregor put her hands on the sides of her chair. Gardner's face made her uneasy. He was too sure of himself, too glib with his answers. She was glad when his face went off and Telford's came back on.

"Dr. Gardner, I've heard the word *epicenter* used in connection with earthquakes. What does the term mean?" Telford asked. Being a good journalist, he knew that his program should inform as well as entertain.

"The epicenter is simply the spot on the earth's surface directly above the point where the earthquake originates. Last night's epicenter was just a bit east of Toronto, under Lake Ontario, as a matter of fact."

"Is it possible to predict earthquakes, Dr. Gardner?"

The professor relit his pipe and shifted his position again.

EPICENTER

The minute hand of the studio clock had swung upward to ten minutes to ten o'clock. The program was due to end at ten. Telford wanted to terminate the interview on a futuristic note, and had skillfully brought the subject around to a point where Gardner could talk about what might lie ahead.

"No. But we're working toward it gradually. But I can tell you here and now that we're due for a major earthquake in the not too distant future." He sniffed the air, and then smacked his lips together.

"How can you be so certain?"

"The law of averages, plus the signs we detect with the new highly sensitive instruments we now have. Twenty years ago —even ten—we used relatively crude instruments to measure quakes. Now we've got extremely sensitive equipment that measures the constant trembling of the earth's crust. When you see these instruments in action you realize that the earth's crust is like a quivering jelly!"

"What type of instrument is this that you've brought along, Dr. Gardner?" Telford asked, taking his cue and pointing to a table on which some equipment was standing. He rose, and this was the prearranged signal for Gardner to rise also and move to the table, the cameras following his pear-shaped form.

"This is a portable seismograph. It's the type we use in our field experiments."

"Will you explain to our viewers how it works? I understand you've rigged it up to record the tremors in the earth outside the studio."

"That's right," Gardner said, and pressed a switch. A large drum started to rotate very slowly on the front of the instrument. Wound around the drum was a sheet of graph paper. A delicate needle slithered and trembled over the surface of the paper, tracing a jagged line about a quarter of an inch from side to side.

"This needle is tracing the tremors from the earth outside," he explained as the cameraman adjusted his zoom lens to create a huge blowup of the needle point and the paper behind it. Gardner pointed his pipe stem at the needle.

He leaned over and turned a knob. Immediately the needle swung violently in wide sweeps from one side of the paper to the other, like a crazy driver weaving a fast car across six lanes of traffic. The zoom lens magnified the effect on television screens. Telford looked up and saw the worried expression on the face of the producer, Jeffries, who was watching the huge zigzags on the monitor in the control room behind the glass partition that separated it from the studio.

"Steady on! That's not a real quake—I hope!" Telford yelled, looking into the camera.

"Oh no," Gardner said calmly, adjusting the knob to reduce the needle's wriggling motions to the quarter-inch quiver. "I'm just showing how we can adjust the wriggle to produce a large-scale effect on the paper. Here's another interesting trick we can do with this instrument. Listen!"

He flicked another switch on the back of the instrument. Instantly a hidden speaker burst out with a "pip-pip-pip-pip" every second. He smiled delightedly, like a child showing off a new toy.

"It's the radio clock from the observatory in Ottawa. I'm regulating the speed of the drum's rotation with the clock. This means we can tell exactly not only where these tremors you see are occurring, but when—right down to a tenth of a second. See, the graph paper is divided into tenths."

"What other instruments do you use besides this type?"

"We record the seismic motion of the earth on tapes and

feed these into a computer. You'd be suprised at the bundles of energy we pick up from all over the world."

Telford glanced at the clock. Two minutes to go.

"All this equipment you've described will help scientists to come up with some method of predicting earthquakes?"

"We hope so."

"What about the aftershock from last night's quake. Is there bound to be an aftershock?" Telford sneaked another look at the clock.

"There's no telling," Gardner replied in a confidential tone. "Matter of fact, we've been wondering about it at the observatory. Sometimes it might take days before it comes. As I said, it can happen any time."

Telford watched the hand of the clock creep toward one minute to ten o'clock. He wanted to end the interview on a climactic note. The program was sponsored by Brimbles New Face Lotion Company, and control would feed in the sponsor's commercial at one minute to ten. He glanced surreptitiously at his notes, searching for a final question to ask Gardner. He hated this moment. There was aways the chance of the interview falling flat on its face, the subject becoming so relieved that the ordeal was nearly over that a reaction set in and he lacked response. But Telford was an old hand at the game. His instinct told him that Gardner was not going to let him down. He would not freeze at the critical moment, which to Telford was the next few seconds of air time.

He need not have worried, for nature worked with him. As Gardner reached across to switch off the portable seismograph, the needle point started to tremble and then swept across the graph paper, quivering like a live thing, tracing a thick jagged line of hills and valleys two inches deep. Telford felt the floor shake, and in one mad moment that forever remained etched in his memory he saw the suspended studio lights sway from side to side. He grasped Gardner's arm. The needle continued to waver and then slowly subside, died to a steady half-inch vibration for a second, then diminished to a normal quiver.

Telford recovered and watched the light on the camera fade, indicating they were off the air. He looked behind the glass at control. Jeffries' face was ash gray, the lines drawn tightly around his mouth as he looked at the monitor. The Brimbles' commercial had hit the air. Then Telford saw Jeffries' face quickly brighten. His mouth relaxed into a grin, and he started to laugh. He swung open the door, rushed into the studio, ran to Gardner standing behind his instrument, and pumped the professor's hand vigorously.

"Wonderful!" he shouted, and then slapped Telford on the back.

The switchboard was quickly jammed with telephone calls. During the last seconds of the interview the television screens of the coast-to-coast network had shown a closeup of the needle slashing from side to side as the aftershock hit southern Ontario. While houses shook and chimneys toppled, viewers saw the live recording of the worst tremor to hit the region in more than a half century. Telford and Gardner grasped the significance of the timing. The professor ran around to the front of the table to get a better view of the instrument, but the needle now jiggled inside its normal limits.

The ten o'clock news was due to follow the commercial. The minute hand swung dead upright, and veteran newscaster Colin Woodman came on the air. After his introductory remarks he went right into the first news item, without looking at the script, making it up as he went along.

"Another earthquake shook Toronto and southern Ontario a few seconds ago. It was an aftershock of the tremor that hit the region less than twenty-four hours ago. By coincidence we had in our studio tonight Dr. Watson A. Gardner, chief of the seismological department of the Dominion Observatory in Ottawa. Dr. Gardner had brought along a portable seismograph to show viewers the natural vibration of the earth. When the quake struck, the instrument happened to be switched on. This is a playback of what viewers saw." Woodman pointed to the controller behind the glass in the news studio.

The videotape flashed on to the monitor. Telford and Gardner, now in the control booth, watched the closeup of the needle swishing from side to side. Telford grasped the desk as he relived the motion when the floor shook. Jeffries, watching the playback, suddenly yelled to Gardner: "How about doing an impromptu right now, explaining what the shock means?" Without waiting for a reply, he grasped Gardner's arm and propelled him next door to the news studio, where Woodman sat before a desk. Jeffries stood just out of camera range, waving his hand to catch Woodman's attention. Woodman looked sideways and realized something important was up. He broke a broadcaster's rule never to let anyone or anything interfere with a newscast, but his quick mind told him what was needed.

". . . just one moment, please. We have with us in the studio Dr. Gardner, who will tell us exactly what happened a few minutes ago and its significance to viewers. Ladies and gentlemen, Dr. Watson A. Gardner, world famous seismologist . . ."

Alice MacGregor picked herself up from the floor where she had crouched when she felt the floor ripple. Her first thought was for her daughter.

"Andy! Andy! Go up and see if Pam's all right. Quick!"

"I'm okay, Mom!" Pamela called from the door. She had run downstairs as soon as she felt the bungalow shake. "But you'd better come and help me clean up the mess in my bedroom. Some of the plaster fell from the ceiling and Ken's picture came off the wall."

"Thank goodness you're all right!" Mrs. MacGregor cried with relief. Then she thought of her husband. Jock had telephoned from the power station early in the morning to say he'd be working a double shift. There was some special work to do and they were short-staffed, but he'd not been more specific. Whatever it was, she wished he'd finish soon and come home.

THREE

The car stopped in front of the carefully plowed snowbank in the parking lot. Johnson had the door open before Townsend switched off the engine. They strode across the open space, their rubbers crunching on the packed snow. It was another one of those clear wintry nights, and the sullen domes of Fairfield's reactor buildings reflected the light from the moon. A fluff of smoke whisked from the squat chimney on the roof of the service building and dissipated into nothingness in the frosty air, and the calm waters of Lake Ontario beyond flickered as the wavelets caught and momentarily held the moonbeams.

The inner guard recognized the two men and let them into the fenced area past the gatehouse. Johnson noticed two ambulances drawn up near the administration building. A short distance away was the station fire truck, its engine running, the crew huddled in the cab trying to keep warm.

The corridor to the control room was endless tonight. It reminded Johnson of the loading bridges airline passengers walked through to board planes, except that this one was interminable. The floor was highly polished but not slippery.

EPICENTER

They walked fast, without speaking, passing a decontamination station set back in the side of the corridor. It had a shower head, a curved tap, and plastic curtains for the modest to hide themselves. A small, finely shaped water basin at the side was designed to wash eyes clear of radioactive material.

The sight of it was a physical reminder to Johnson of the inherent hazards involved in the generation of electricity from nuclear power and, in particular, the siting of atomic stations close to big cities. He recalled the discussions that had taken place at some of the conferences he'd attended of the Canadian Nuclear Association and the Atomic Industrial Forum in New York, and the various viewpoints put forward when some of the two countries' leading experts discussed the problem and how they had agreed that there was no real danger if proper safety precautions were taken. He remembered the weeks immediately following the opening of the station and, curiously, the smell of the new vinyl tile in the control room as he'd explained to a group of visiting Members of Parliament the stringent safety precautions designed into the station.

"There's never been a case of death—or even injury—to a member of the public caused by accidents to any nuclear power station," he'd said. They crowded around him as he stood with his back to the control console. He paused, and opened his mouth to continue when a stony-faced woman from an eastern Ontario township spoke up in a shrill voice. She wasn't an MP but a town councillor who had attached herself, uninvited, to the group of visiting dignitaries.

"It's madness to put a potential atom bomb only a few miles from a built-up area!" she said icily.

Johnson stared at her, consciously controlling his irritation.

"A nuclear power station works on an entirely different principle from an atom bomb," he said evenly, and then proceeded to explain the difference in lay language.

31

"But isn't Fairfield the first large nuclear station that's been built so close to a big center of population?" His questioner was a big raw-featured man from a western Canada constituency who had a raspy voice and the look of the open prairie about him. He moved awkwardly in his tailored suit, tugging at the sleeves and hefting his shoulders. "You said yourself it's only about twenty miles to downtown Toronto," he continued.

"Yes—that's just what I was going to ask!" the waspish woman cried stridently.

"The locations of nuclear power stations are rigidly controlled by the Atomic Energy Control Board in Ottawa, under the Atomic Control Act," Johnson replied. "The board has a safety committee to advise on all the safety aspects. These people are top scientists, mostly from federal government agencies. And there are local representatives from health and labor organizations on the committee."

"Did you say *labor?*" the tall man asked. By the way he spoke Johnson had the feeling he was a pro-union man.

"Yes. There are more than 240 people working in this power station. Every precaution is taken for their safety—"

"That's all very well—" the woman cut in. He ignored her and continued.

"This station has a new type of safety control system built into it so that if anything went wrong—a most unlikely event —the whole of the radioactive section could be completely isolated in a few seconds. Before any leak of radioactive material could occur we'd get advance notice on this computer over here."

He nodded at the computer console in the corner of the room and ten heads swiveled obediently.

"As a matter of fact, if a leak did occur, the computer would automaticaly shut down the station."

EPICENTER

They'd seemed satisfied. He had had the feeling, as he spoke to them later when he guided them around other parts of the station, that as MP's they didn't want to show their ignorance of the complex workings of the station by asking too many questions. And if Ottawa had authorized the station to be built so close to a large city, then it must be all right.

They passed another decontamination shower near the control room, and Johnson's mind jerked back to the present. One o'clock in the morning was a hell of a time to be roused from a warm bed and told about more damage to the station due to the aftershock, especially after being on duty all through the previous night and most of the following day. Both he and Townsend had been exhausted, with Townsend in a state of collapse. Johnson had ordered him to go home and rest, and the relief-shift controller had firmly suggested that Johnson do the same. Reluctantly he'd had to admit he was all in, and went home, leaving strict instructions to be called immediately if conditions deteriorated.

Earlier in the day he had organized a team to find the missing bundles. MacGregor used geiger counters along the chute where it came through the reactor-building wall and dropped in a rapid slope to the underground water tank. The counters clicked wildly at a point near the ground where the chute curved before dropping into the tank. Although separated by the steel chute and concrete, the needle on the geiger counter swung swiftly up the scale. MacGregor fell back. He reasoned that the two bundles were in the chute together, one on top of the other, but he wasn't sure. The chances were that they would be together because it was not likely that the bundles had jammed at separate points in the chute. A conference had been hurriedly called. Johnson explained the position.

"It's possible the two bundles are angled slightly, end to

end. The ends might be touching. This would crank them up so that the opposite ends rub against the sides of the chute." He spoke quietly but his voice had a slight huskiness. On a paper pad he sketched a portion of the chute and drew in two oblongs to represent the bundles.

"If we refuel another tube and discharge one bundle down the chute, it might have enough energy to push the two stuck bundles along," MacGregor suggested.

Johnson covered his face with his hands. He rubbed his eyes. It was a good idea, but there was the risk of ending up with three stuck bundles instead of two. He looked at MacGregor and pressed his lips together. MacGregor knew instinctively he'd already thought of the idea and had rejected it.

"How about tackling the problem from the other end?" Townsend suggested. "The bundles are at the point where the chute starts to level off before entering the water tank. Perhaps it's possible for the remotely operated crane in the tank to reach the end of the lower bundle and jerk it forward."

Johnson's face brightened. It might work, if the crane had sufficient travel to swing forward far enough to swipe the end of the fuel bundles.

"Get the handbook on the waste fuel tank," he ordered. An operator ran to the bookcase on the far side of the control room and returned with a thick volume.

Johnson flipped through the sections and studied the plan that showed how far the crane could swing. The crane's range was far too short.

"It won't reach. Good try." He forced a smile in Townsend's direction.

At one point he thought of shutting down the reactor they had started to refuel. He suggested it to Townsend and the control room engineer but they decided that such a drastic measure was unnecessary. It would reduce the power output of the station and not in any way solve the basic problem of dislodging the fuel bundles and their deadly radioactive load. When the relief-shift controller came on duty at dawn—an experienced man responsible for the control room staff—a quick discussion took place. It was decided to trace the chute farther down toward the water tank to try to get an exact fix on the bundles. It was at this point that the shift controller had firmly suggested that Johnson and Townsend get some rest.

When the call came through after the second earthquake shock, Johnson suddenly remembered his car was out of commission. Taxi service was unreliable where he lived, so he arranged to have Townsend pick him up since he lived not far away.

Townsend reached the double swinging doors of the control room first and swung one door open for Johnson. The group of men crowded around the console looked up as they entered. Johnson's eyes were immediately drawn to the two television monitors, two automated cold eyes that stared malignantly at the humans in the room, The controller stood at the console. When he saw Johnson a wave of relief swept over his face.

"Is the reactor building still isolated?" Johnson demanded. He'd asked the same question when the telephone's piercing sound had awakened him from slumbers so deep that even the aftershock, although it rocked his apartment building, had failed to disturb him.

"Yes. All airlocks are still shut."

"What's the air pressure in the reactor building?"

"Normal."

He'd worried about the air pressure. Some vague warning at the back of his mind told him it was important.

"Where's the emergency team?" he asked.

"On standby in the service building. They've located the bundles in the chute above grade level, where the bend is."

"Good old Jock!" Johnson exclaimed. A smile hovered on his face, then vanished.

He looked up at the television screens. The fueling machines stood immobile: inanimate mocking monsters surrounded by a strange aura of vindictiveness. In the right-hand screen he could see the dark shadow where the upper end of the chute emerged near the machine. It looked so simple. All he had to do was ram a long spiral plumbing wire down that opening and give the bundles a push . . .

"We'd better move down to the chute near the water tank," he said. "Any structural damage to the buildings?"

"There's a crack in the concrete footings near the chute. MacGregor says the geiger count is zero along the crack, but high where the bundles are stuck. It may have opened up with the aftershock."

One of the telephones on the desk rang shrilly and an operator picked it up. "It's for you, sir. Ottawa," he said, handing the instrument to Johnson.

The lines around his jaw creased into tight crevices as he listened. The room, already silent, fell into an even quieter hush. Johnson's eyes focused on some spot on the ceiling. He nodded his head. When he spoke his voice perked up.

"No structural damage. A slight crack along the concrete footing near the chute. We were refueling at the time the first tremor struck. That's right. Two fuel bundles failed to show up on the inspection table in the underground water tank.

EPICENTER

We think we've located them. They're stuck between the refueling machine and the tank, near the bend in the chute.
We're just going to do another inspection. So far there's no
leak of any sort, but the geiger reading where the bundles are
stuck is above normal."

Johnson had recognized the crisp staccato voice immediately. Richard A. Deighton, scientific director, Atomic Energy
Control Board, had a peculiar cadence to his speech, a firm
roundness. Deighton, a leading international nuclear physicist,
had been visiting lecturer on the course Johnson had taken on
nuclear power station operation. Johnson remembered his
tremendous energy and enthusiasm. He'd lecture by day on
the complexities of nuclear reactors, work on a research paper
until the small hours, and be first in the breakfast hall at seven
the next morning, eager and ready to go. He was a man with
a distinguished career in his chosen field, with a curriculum
vitae in the records of AECB seven pages long, and in his
youth had been a science honors graduate who'd carried off
the Governor General's Prize for three years in a row, a record never since equaled. He listened as Deighton spoke.

"I was wondering about the airflow, too. I'll report back
as soon as possible. All right, sir," Johnson said, hanging up.

"That was Deighton at AECB. He wants a full report by
phone on the condition of the footings of the chute."

He looked around the room, nodded at Townsend, and
said, "You'd better come along." He picked up the telephone
and asked MacGregor to meet him in the compartment where
the chute emerged from the reactor building. They took
white coveralls from the wall and put respirators over their
faces. He checked that Townsend was wearing his radiation
exposure badge on the front of the coveralls.

The smooth gray concrete walls oppressed Johnson. The

glaring lights set in the ceiling defined every wrinkle in their surfaces. He looked at MacGregor and his emergency team, dressed in plastic protective suits with the hoods lying back on their shoulders, respirators in position. MacGregor's suit, which had been developed especially for this work, had a transparent visor that covered his face, and a roll of rubber hose for breathing and cooling air was looped neatly on his belt. The suit enabled MacGregor to enter areas at the station where the air was both hot and filled with contaminated particles of dust, but it did not offer protection against deadly gamma rays, which could penetrate practically anything except thick lead or dense concrete. Lengths of rubber hose could be connected together to allow him to extend the range of his operations. The suit did the basic job admirably, but it had one major disadvantage. The cool air swiftly burbling through the suit was noisy and interfered with the wearer's hearing. A sound-barrier type of earphone, similar to those worn by ground crews working around jet aircraft, had been tried, but the noise problem had still not been solved.

The little group stood in a large cell-like structure near the thick protective wall of the reactor building, at ground level looking at the doors of the airlock before them that permanently sealed off the inside of the reactor building from the rest of the station. On the far side of the structure was a slanting concrete shape—the outline of the chute leading to the water tank. Johnson looked at it intently. It appeared innocuous enough. A geiger counter stood on one side, which MacGregor had placed there during his first survey, and a red chalk mark outlined the radioactive area. Across the smooth concrete floor another heavy chalk mark indicated the point beyond which it was unsafe to approach the chute. Johnson bent to check the reading on the nearest geiger counter. MacGregor came up to him. "There's an inspection panel on the top face of the chute just there, sir," he told Johnson. "It was sealed after construction, but I could get it open and stick a probe rod in and give the bundles a push."

Johnson stared at him. "What about radiation? As soon as you raise the panel you'd be exposed," he said, his voice muffled by the respirator.

"No sir!" MacGregor replied, tossing his head. The confidence in his voice negated what would in normal circumstances have been a rude contradiction.

"That panel's very thick," he continued, and moved his hands about three feet apart. "An' that's solid concrete. Plus the fact the air in this chamber would be drawn into the reactor building once I got it open. The air pressure's 'igher 'ere so the air would flow away from us."

Johnson thought for a moment, mentally tracing a blueprint before replying. "At this point there isn't much difference between the pressures, but enough to prevent air coming from the reactor building," he admitted, but there was doubt in his voice.

He turned to Townsend. "The panel Jock's referring to was put in to inspect the inside of the chute after it was completed. It's about three feet long and two wide. It's over there, on the upper surface of the shielding on the chute." He pointed and took a step in the direction of the chute.

The portion of the chute Johnson indicated was about halfway up the wall, about eight feet above the floor and approximately six feet below the ceiling. The idea seemed highly dangerous to Townsend. If the panel were removed, air would be sucked into the opening in the chute and rush into the reactor building. That wasn't the worry. The big question was how much radiation would shoot through the opening when the panel was lifted off. It could expose them to an excessive dose of gamma rays from the decaying waste-fuel bundles.

Townsend instinctively fingered the film badge pinned to his coveralls. He longed to check its color, although his intellect told him it showed normal, but he didn't want the others to see. For the first time he noticed that MacGregor carried a radiation dosemeter, a sensitive instrument for measuring doses absorbed by a person working close to nuclear equipment, and he suddeny felt chilled.

"What about the danger from gamma rays?" Townsend said at length.

"The panel will be eased up just enough to get the probe in," Johnson replied. "There'll be no escape of air from the reactor building. The suction will be the other way—from here to there."

He looked along the concrete shielding on the chute and approached the surface with a geiger counter. No change in the count occurred when he held the instrument near. There was a faint hairline crack for about six feet along the concrete, near the floor.

"It's difficult to know whether that's always been there," Townsend said over his shoulder. "It could have been caused by a slight settlement of the building or it could have been the aftershock."

Johnson touched the crack with his gloved fingers. "The surface edges seem fresh, but with concrete that smooth you can't tell. MacGregor said he couldn't remember either. I'm going to call Deighton," he said decisively. He stood up and went to the door.

While he was gone the others stood around in little knots, nerves edgy. Witzensky, MacGregor's right-hand man, conferred with the stubby red-haired Scot in earnest tones.

EPICENTER

Townsend sat on an upturned wooden box, shut his eyes, and reviewed the diagram that spread across his mind's eye. He hadn't known about the inspection panel; it had been permanently sealed after the station had been constructed and had no servicing or maintenance function. An uneasy feeling settled at the back of his mind.

Johnson returned, a little brighter. "Deighton's okayed the idea. He thinks the cracks are old settlement lines," he said. He looked up at the ceiling above the chute. "We're going to need a pulley block and hoist, some ladders and planks to make a platform," he told MacGregor, the confident ring of command returning to his voice.

MacGregor dispatched men to bring the material and equipment. He instructed Witzensky to anchor the pulley block and its long chain to a steel beam that protruded from the ceiling above the chute. Townsend got station handbook Volume Seven, *Structural*, from the control room and Johnson opened it and turned to a big folder tucked in a pocket inside the stiff back cover. He got down on his knees and spread a blueprint over the floor. Townsend and MacGregor bent over him.

"The panel's here." Johnson pointed to the rectangular outline among the pattern of white lines on the blue background. "That puts it six feet from that wall," he said, pointing.

MacGregor measured the distance with a steel rule, drew a chalk mark, and approached the concrete covering the chute. He glanced at the dosimeter clipped to his suit and walked closer, adjusting the narrow plank in his hand to the chalk mark.

"It'll be 'ere, Arnie," he called to Witzensky. "Get the ladder under it. I'll put a chalk mark on the shielding."

Witzensky motioned to one of the men to move the ladder

into position. The team quickly assembled a platform of planks around the chute, and the pulley block and chain swung from the horizontal beam directly over the chalk mark.

The panel had been cemented into position. It had a recessed steel bar on the upper surface to form a handle. MacGregor climbed up the ladder, stood on the shielding, and put a cold chisel and hammer to the cement at the panel edges. A shower of mortar chips fell at Johnson's feet. MacGregor's short, bent-up figure reminded him of a dwarf hammering at a gargoyle on some Gothic cathedral. MacGregor whisked away the fine powder that had accumulated in the crevice he'd chiseled.

"That's it!" he shouted. His head peered over the chute. "I think it'll come away easy now!"

Johnson called out: "You'd better put your hood on, Jock. We'll connect you to the cooling air for safety."

MacGregor threw down the end of the hose he'd uncoiled from his waist. Someone grabbed it and connected it to a cold-air outlet on the wall. "Okay, let 'er rip!" he yelled, his voice muffled by the visor. The man slowly unscrewed the valve, and the air started to fill MacGregor's suit. He made a shivering gesture, and a big grin spread across his face under the visor. Johnson looked stern. He didn't like the offhand attitude, but he knew MacGregor was nervously reacting to the dangerous job ahead. MacGregor adjusted the valve at his waist, enough to keep the air circulating at low speed through the suit.

Johnson thought about the report he'd read in the library when he first went to training school. The accident to the NRX reactor at Atomic Energy of Canada's research place at Chalk River in the early days must have resembled this tense scene. The reactor had actually run away—been out of control for a few seconds—and suddenly flared into a hundred million watts of heat. The report had spoken about the dedication to duty by the men called out on the emergency. There'd been no panic. By the time the chief executives of Atomic Energy had arrived on the scene pipelines had been laid from the basement of the reactor to carry off the radio-active heavy water to a shielded storage tank where it could do no harm. It took fourteen months to get the reactor back to normal operation. Personnel from the Canadian Armed Forces and radiation experts from the United States Atomic Energy Commission had rushed to help.

He drew a deep breath and let it escape through the respirator in a long sigh. MacGregor had climbed on top of the shielding that covered the chute and was fastening a huge hook to the panel handle. He checked the geiger counter.

"It's okay," he called to Johnson. "Give me the rod."

Witzensky and a workman passed him a long steel rod. MacGregor grasped it firmly with both hands and placed it on the shielding and then gripped the chain that ran through the pulleys and pulled slowly to take up the slack. The panel was exactly three feet thick, corresponding to the thickness of the concrete shielding, and attached to its lower surface was a thick steel panel in the chute itself.

"Better put another counter on each side of the opening. Stand 'em on the planks," he shouted to Johnson, who waved to the men. They strained to lift the heavy instruments above their heads, and MacGregor slid them into position. Satisfied, he held the chain and applied pressure to pull it through the pulleys. The tightly fitted panel didn't budge. He knelt down and swept his hands over the crack. It had lifted a fraction of an inch. He pulled again. The panel edged upward, standing slightly higher than the shielding surface. MacGregor paused. The geiger counters ticked in a regular but slow rhythm. He yanked carefully on the chain. The panel rose about half an inch. With each foot of chain that he swept through the pulley system, the panel rose higher, until about eighteen inches of the tapered concrete appeared. Now every time the chain stopped rattling through the pulleys Johnson could hear the ping-ping of the counters accelerate, but Mac-Gregor seemed not to notice—perhaps the sound was muffled by the cooling air rushing past his ears. The panel was three-quarters free of the opening, and twisted slightly as it rotated. MacGregor steadied it with the toe of his boot.

"Keep away!" Johnson shouted.

"It's okay," MacGregor yelled. "The edge of the panel's shielding my foot." He glanced down at the upraised strained faces.

"What do the indicators show?" Johnson called out, listening to the chorus of pinging counters.

"About halfway up the scale."

Johnson calculated the emission. Not critical yet. The rapid ping-ping was deceptive. He nodded at Townsend. MacGregor stopped, waiting for an opinion.

"Slowly—really slowly now!" Johnson called. "If it swings sideways again use this to keep it straight." He held up a piece of wood. MacGregor took it and started to pull the chain very slowly. The panel was about two-thirds up from its seating. An opening four inches wide appeared between it and the fixed part of the shielding, too narrow to insert the steel rod. He moved one counter nearer to the opening, placing it between his body and the widening aperture. It clicked rapidly. Everything was now set for the final lifting stage.

He pulled, a long steady heave. The taper on the lower part of the panel slanted at a sharp angle. Another pull. He could see the glint of metal as the thick steel cover caught the light. The counters sang out louder, like babbling old women. He glanced at the instrument near his feet. The needle was over the halfway mark. Another pull. The steel plate was almost clear of the opening. A long, slow, steady yank and the metal cleared the hole, swaying slightly. He judged that another inch would be enough to get the rod to pass through almost horizontally, perhaps at a low enough angle to reach the bundles. The panel could remain where it was, suspended by the hook and chain. He moved away from the opening, standing upright on the shielding. For the first time Mac-Gregor was conscious of the sweat congealing inside the plastic suit, and he turned up the cold-air regulator at his belt. He gave the thumbs-up sign to Johnson.

"Have a rest, Jock," Johnson shouted, his shoulders hunched despite his upturned head. MacGregor didn't reply, swung down the ladder, and paced up and down on the floor. Johnson saw the blue eyes narrow as MacGregor thought about his next move.

"Need any help with the rod?" Johnson asked.

MacGregor unhinged the transparent visor. "I can manage myself, sir," he replied, and refastened the headpiece. Escaping air hissed through an aperture. His eyes glistened. He was anxious to get the job finished, but he knew that he must not be tempted to hurry.

He mounted the ladder and Witzensky held the rubber hose high to keep it from snagging. Standing on top of the shielding, MacGregor picked up the rod and pointed the end toward the opening, holding it horizontally. He moved it hand over hand until he stood about six feet away from the hole. He had to tip the rod to pry it under the thick panel with its steel bottom plate. Slowly he fed it through steady gloved hands under the massive block and into the chute. There was a sharp metallic clang. The rod had hit the opposite edge of the panel opening, where a steel frame for the metal part of the panel had been molded into the concrete. Mac-

Gregor gingerly prized up the end of the rod. It wouldn't budge.

He'd have to raise the panel higher. He pulled out the rod, settled it on the shielding, and moved the geiger counter closer to the opening. He put his hand on the chain and pulled down. The concrete panel hefted upward half an inch, but still not high enough for the rod to pass. He applied pressure again. The panel moved another half inch. He glanced at the counter. The needle moved upward, nearing the red danger line. He picked up the rod, inserted the end in the opening, and carefully thrust it forward into the chute. This time it cleared the opposite end of the opening, but he had to tilt it so that the end would not hit the bottom of the chute. The rod had gone in only about four feet. He put his weight behind it, but it wouldn't move.

Johnson waved for him to stop. It was going to be tougher than they had thought. MacGregor balanced the rod between the panel edge and the chute, holding the end lightly in his hand. Johnson made a movement to show that the rod would have to be bent. MacGregor withdrew it, skillfully drawing it close to the counter to monitor the amount of radiation it had picked up, which was negligible. The flow of air from the room into the chute was toward the reactor building, the bulky form at the back of the room, and any radioactive dust on the rod had been carried in that direction. He handed the rod to Witzensky and his helpers, who took it to the service shop.

The next time MacGregor approached the opening in the chute the rod was bowed, and the arched portion fitted snugly under the suspended panel. Without taking his eyes off the rod, he nodded to those on the floor that all was well. He pushed forward. The rod hit something solid.

"That's it," he yelled into the visor, steadying the end of

the rod. His boots were about three feet from the opening. He looked at the anxious faces below and nodded vigorously. The moment for applying force to the bundles had arrived. MacGregor needed help. He moved his head to tell Witzensky that he wanted him on the shielding. Witzensky, awkward in his plastic suit, lumbered up the ladder and positioned himself behind MacGregor. The two men grasped the rod and pushed. Nothing happened. The bundles were firmly stuck in the chute. The rod, although bowed, rubbed against the underside of the panel, which swayed with their exertions. They pushed again. It was clear the panel would have to be pulled higher to give enough clearance. MacGregor bent down and peered into the opening to see how much more he'd have to lift the panel.

"Get away, Jock!" Johnson yelled.

MacGregor couldn't hear. As he stooped, the heavy sleeve of his suit snagged the control knob of the air valve and turned it up high, and the air raced through the suit, roaring past his ear like a miniature tornado. He lifted his hand to grip the knob, faltered, and lost his balance. He fell forward on his knees, his right hand hitting the panel as it swayed on the end of the chain. For one horrible moment he was poised directly over the opening with his left hand gripping the edge of the chute.

Witzensky dashed forward, grasped his chief's shoulders, and pulled him back. He glanced at the counter at MacGregor's feet. The needle had run off the scale and was hard against the upper stop.

Jock MacGregor, aged forty-seven, nuclear service technician chief, had just been killed.

He struggled to his feet, grasped the rod, and withdrew it completely. He laid it on the shielding and waved for Witzensky to jump down. Witzensky tried to pull him away, but

MacGregor shook him off. He ran forward and pulled the chain through the well-oiled pulleys as fast as he could, lowering the panel into the opening. His disciplined mind told him exactly what he must do. He knew, too, that his body had shielded Witzensky from the deadly gamma rays that had shot out of the enlarged opening. The chain rattled and went slack as the panel clumped shut, and those below rushed to help MacGregor climb down the ladder.

FOUR

By eight thirty that same morning the nails on MacGregor's left hand—the one that had grasped the opening of the chute—turned black. The two nurses in the sealed-off hospital room went about their duties in silence. Alice MacGregor, Johnson, and Townsend sat in the corridor outside, waiting for the radiation biologists to make their report. Johnson watched a white-clad orderly wheel some instruments into the room, but the door closed too soon for him to see anything inside.

In an adjoining room the doctor in charge studied the little pile of metallic odds and ends he had taken from MacGregor's clothing. A gold-plated tieclip—a Father's Day present from Andy—two dimes and a quarter, the zipper from his pants, a belt buckle, ballpoint pen, and the metal fittings from the plastic suit. He passed them under a proportional counter, an instrument that measured tiny amounts of radiation. He hoped it would yield some clue to the massive dosage MacGregor had been exposed to in the short time he was poised over the opening. He shook his head slowly.

"Don't think it's any use," he whispered to the biologist at his side, and pushed the metal pieces away.

EPICENTER

He needn't have spoken in such a low voice. Through a long oblong window he could see MacGregor sitting up in bed in the next room: the window was one-way glass. To MacGregor it was a long mirror on the wall opposite his bed. The doctor looked intently at MacGregor, whose face was curiously solemn as he peered at his fingernails. The fingers and thumb of the left hand had reddened and were growing fat, and the same change was occurring to his right hand but at a slower rate.

Radiation absorption in living tissue was measured in RADs, Radiation Absorbed Dose. Damage from radiation tended to be cumulative, which was one reason why everybody working at Fairfield and other nuclear stations had to wear film badges—photographic film specially adapted to measure radioactivity collected over a period of time. Several thousand RADs would kill a person whether he was exposed in a second or over many years. The maximum lifetime dose that radiation biologists considered safe—with certain reservations—was 250 RADs. Workers in nuclear stations, and then only those whose work brought them close to a radioactive source, were sometimes exposed to only millirads (thousandths of a RAD) of radiation an hour, an insignificant amount compared with the fatal dose. The radiation dose was substantially lessened the farther the recipient was from a source.

MacGregor had received in those lethal five or six seconds a massive dose—more than 10,000 RADs—within three yards of the source, and his exposure had been to gamma rays given off by the unburned plutonium in the spent fuel bundles, one of the most intense of all types of radiation. Gamma rays carry such a powerful charge of energy that when they hit human or animal tissue they cause changes not only to the molecules of the cells but to the atoms making up the molecules. The energy breaks down the cell structure: it destroys the living tissue by disintegration. Even if a person receives even a relatively slight exposure to gamma rays and successfully recovers, he still runs the chance that his sex cells have been so damaged that his offspring could be mutated—born as a monstrosity, malformed, sickeningly unshaped as a human being.

The doctor went out into the corridor through a side entrance and closed the door quietly. Johnson studied his face. There was a note of sadness in the way the doctor stood.

"You know how much exposure he had," the medic said, addressing the two men, his mellow voice low. He turned to Alice MacGregor and said compassionately, "I'm sorry. All we can do is relieve his suffering."

She put a wet handkerchief to her eyes and sobbed quietly. It was so final, so fatalistic, that Johnson suddenly felt the air turn evil. A queer spasm shot through his body. He fought for breath.

"You may go in now," the doctor said.

"All of us?" Townsend asked.

The doctor nodded. "We'll come in in a few minutes, Mrs. MacGregor," Johnson said. She put away the handkerchief, blinked her eyes, and pushed under her Sunday hat the stray curls that had fallen out of place. When she went into the room she was smiling.

Johnson silently closed the door and sat on the wooden bench in the corridor. The door suddenly opened and Alice MacGregor appeared. She had taken off her heavy winter coat, revealing a plain dark blue suit, but was still wearing her Sunday hat.

"Come in. Jock said he wants to see you."

"Hi, Jock," Johnson said, forcing his face into a smile. He noticed the two nurses in a corner of the big room.

"You'll have to move those ruddy bundles on your own!" MacGregor said resonantly.

Johnson recovered from the smothering sensation. When he spoke his voice was normal. It seemed safest to talk shop.

"When you had the rod against the bundles what d'you think was stopping them from being moved?"

"I think it was just their weight. They're heavy y' know. I think if three men got on the pushing end we could do it." MacGregor spoke deliberately. Although he included himself, he knew he was dying and would never again enter Fairfield. He looked at his hands, drawing the attention of his visitors to the blackened nails and puffy flesh. Johnson passed a handkerchief over his forehead. Alice MacGregor, seated at the head of the bed, bit her bottom lip.

The white-clad doctor, standing near the window, said, "I think it's time to leave. We mustn't tire him. You can come back this afternoon."

Six hours later MacGregor's hands were so painfully swollen that they had to be wrapped in ice. The doctor administered morphine. The redness had also appeared on MacGregor's chest and lower abdomen. His eyes became puffy. Ulcers had appeared in his mouth.

Despite his pain he was cheerful when Johnson saw him that evening. He'd asked for a report on Witzensky, who'd been taken to the same hospital and discharged after close examination but told to stay at home and rest for a couple of days. Defying instructions, he was at that very minute driving to the hospital to visit MacGregor.

The cells of living tissue are tough. They struggle to function properly after being attacked, and some semblance of normality returns as they fight back while trying feverishly to reproduce themselves. By the time Witzensky saw Mac-Gregor he was sitting up again eating an evening meal with obvious enjoyment, fed to him by a nurse.

But nature was laying a trail of camouflaged hopes. By midnight blisters had formed on MacGregor's swollen hands, the skin was taut, and the swelling had extended to his left forearm. At daybreak the blisters—huge elemental angry conglomerations of fluid under tightly drawn scarlet skin—had appeared on both arms and his chest. MacGregor's face turned a muddy color and his forehead swelled in yellow blotches. He had vomited the meal he had eaten the previous evening, and he continued to gag and belch through the morning. By one o'clock the retching stopped. His tufty red hair became brittle, and when he elbowed up from the pillow patches of dry wiry strands stuck to the linen.

Despite the slow decomposition of his body, MacGregor's mind stayed alert. He grinned when Witzensky and Johnson lined up in the next room to donate blood for transfusions. He didn't know that Pamela had also given blood and that Andy had volunteered but had been turned down because he was too young.

The doctor worried about the blood count—the white corpuscles were not reproducing at their normal rate. He ordered a regular count to be made frequently.

During the evening of the first day MacGregor asked one of the nurses to prop him up so that he could read the evening papers someone had brought, but he found it too painful to turn the pages.

"Make y'self useful, lassie," he said, nodding his head in a way she understood. She sat on the edge of the bed, turning the pages at his request.

"They've managed to keep it out of the papers, then," he said laconically. His voice was strong, but a sudden wave of pain overtook him, forcing him to lie down.

When Johnson saw him at nine thirty the next morning his condition had deteriorated further. His fingernails had turned an angry blackish purple and his hands looked like blown-up tomatoes. He was propped up in bed, his eyes glittering.

"You could get the bundles out by rolling a round lead weight down the opening!" he said authoritatively. "It doesn't matter if the weight gets into the water tank. Just leave it there."

"Still working!" Johnson said, with awe in his voice. "What're you trying to do, run up overtime?"

"Aye—that's it! Time and a 'alf! It's the union rate!"

Johnson went along with the kidding. He had come for a reason grimmer than to trade jokes, but he hesitated. Late the previous night he'd spoken to the doctor on the telephone. Death was near. The biologists had met that same afternoon, considered every facet, explored every possibility of hope.

"Jock," Johnson said, his voice wavering. "I was wondering if there's anything I can do—like help Alice or the kids. Anything."

"That's very considerate of you, sir, but I think everything's gonna be all right. I've put away a bit and there's the insurance and—"

Johnson turned to the window. There was a long silence in the room.

"I think Mr. MacGregor's got to have his rest before his transfusion. It'll be all right for you to see him this afternoon," the nurse said quietly.

Two days later, after examining the blood count a nurse had taken, the doctor sucked in his breath. The white corpuscles were dying. Their reproductive ability had ended.

EPICENTER

MacGregor's body was now degenerating rapidly. His ulcerated mouth was painful, his tongue swollen. The next morning, when Witzensky visited him, MacGregor's limp form lay beneath the sheets, just his face and almost-bald scalp visible. His eyes were bright, but he spoke with great pain.

Alice MacGregor, who had been allowed to sleep in an adjoining room, was sitting at his bedside. Her cheeks were gray hollows and her eyes had the look of a cheated person, hurt and with a bitter anger kept under control.

The doctor appeared in the doorway. "I don't think you should tax him too much. Sit with him but don't make him talk," he said.

MacGregor muttered something unintelligible and his eyelids fluttered. Alice MacGregor called for the doctor to come quickly.

"It's all right," he reassured her. "He's in a coma. There— listen to what he's saying."

She bent close. "Round 'eads go in this box an' countersunk 'eads 'ere—" MacGregor said distinctly before his voice trailed off into a raspy sound. She looked up at the doctor with a puzzled expression.

"Often patients dream about something that happened a long time ago when they go into coma. He might be dreaming about something that happened to him as a child. He'll be okay."

Witzensky crept out of the room. Alice MacGregor bent over the pillow, listening to the voice of her husband as distant memory awakened in the brain cells that were beginning to be attacked. He was back in his teen-age days, and parading before the backdrop of his memory were the events of his first day as an apprentice in the Clyde shipyards, before the days of all-welded ships.

He'd begun work in the predawn light at six thirty that

day, as a rivet sorter. The different types of rivets were sorted into metal boxes where they were stored. His young heart sank when the chargehand led him to a cask filled with odd rivets that had been thrown into it; he had expected to start work as a helper to an engine room fitter.

" 'Ere, sort 'em out! Round 'eads go in this box an' countersunk 'eads 'ere. If you find any mushroom 'eads stick 'em 'ere."

MacGregor sat on an upturned empty barrel for ten hours and sorted rivets. The next day he did the same thing. By the third day he could see the bottom of the cask. By midafternoon the job had been completed. On that day he discovered an important principle.

The chargehand came to inspect his progress, and looked at the boxes of carefully sorted rivets. He peered into the depths of the empty cask, his eyes opened wide with astonishment, and a grin slowly spread across his craggy face.

"Well done, laddie! You're too good for this job. How'd you like to work in the engine machine shop?"

MacGregor was too staggered to believe what he heard. He rubbed his dirty hands on the backsides of his newly starched brown overalls.

"I'd like that, sir," he said quietly. The chargehand led him away. The other apprentices looked up from their work with cool eyes that showed a mixture of envy and interest.

The chargehand took him out of the fitting shop, along the length of the shipyard where the steel skeleton of a ship under construction stood in a kind of naked glory, and ducked through a door into the machine shop. MacGregor's eyes were filled with wonder and anticipation. He looked with awe at the whirling milling machines, rotating lathes and huge jig borers mounted in ranks that seemed to disappear into the distance in the vast shop. Spirals of bright swarf churned from the cutting tools and soapy lubricating water splashed on the floor. He smelled the smell of the machine shop: acrid, metally. The chargehand took him into a glass-fronted office overlooking the shop.

"This is young MacGregor, as good an apprentice as I ever set eyes on. 'E's too good for dead-end jobs," the chargehand said to old MacPherson, the foreman.

"Aye? We'll see what he can do, then," MacPherson said loudly, a habit he'd developed in the noisy shop, looking piercingly at the wide-eyed boy before him.

Twelve months later MacGregor was awarded the apprentice-of-the-year prize, five Scottish pound notes and a framed certificate. When the general manager of the shipyard presented it to him he was too overcome to say more than "Thank you, sir."

"Thank—you—sir," MacGregor muttered, and his eyes flickered open. His wife put out her hand to smooth his forehead, damp with perspiration.

The next day his body started to turn an angry dark purple and the yellow blotches on his skin took on a grimmer tone. His digestive system collapsed, and he had to be fed intravenously. At the same time his stomach and intestines had to be drained through a plastic tube pushed up his nose and down his now ulcerating throat. The doctor ordered him placed in an oxygen tent. Alice MacGregor stoically sat by the plastic-covered bed. MacGregor's body was an aggregation of cellular decay. The basic structure of the millions of cells that comprised his flesh had collapsed. The destruction was in its final stages. When MacGregor slowly turned his face to his wife he groped to recognize her. The attack on the nervous system was affecting his brain. His lips had turned purple, and they struggled to pronounce something. Alice bent close to the transparent tent to hear, but the words came as a meaningless sigh.

"I think you'd better leave him now." The doctor who'd been watching close behind hurried to the tent. "He can't understand you. He's lapsed into a coma again."

He died that same day, before the light went from the western sky. By eight o'clock the little room had been cleared, except for a small collection of metallic objects—a gold-plated tieclip, two dimes and a quarter—which the orderly who maintained the room had overlooked.

FIVE

Johnson peered through the visor at the shielding surrounding the chute. The others stood behind him. The air circulating in the suit blasted his ears and magnified the crunching noises as the plastic bent with the movements of his body. The needle of the portable geiger counter he carried hovered at the red danger mark.

He turned to Townsend, making a helpless gesture with his shoulders, and tossed his head sideways, indicating a movement away from the chamber. The hooded figures moved outside, and Johnson carefully pulled the rubber air hoses through the door. He turned off the air supply and the hissing around his ears stopped.

"Too hot in there! The radioactivity level's climbing! Let's get back to control," he commanded, raising the visor.

But control came to them in the form of a breathless technician. He appeared on the steps leading down to the chamber.

"Telephone's out of order, sir. We couldn't reach you!" he yelled. "The poison-leak dial shows above normal, sir. We thought it could get into the station ventilation system!"

Johnson felt his skin go cold. He led the charge up the

steps, through the doorway at the top, and into the administration wing. Someone was holding the swinging doors of the control room open.

"Townsend, get an air sampler fixed up in this room!" Johnson ordered. He turned to the shift boss. "Are all the station phones out of order?"

"Only some. I think there's a line under the chute. It must have—"

"Test the central PA system. Make certain it's working in all parts of the station," Johnson ordered, taking a necessary precaution.

Townsend brought in an air sampler and placed it in the middle of the room. Johnson looked at the gauges. The leak detection pointers for Number One reactor had leapt from their zero lines and were standing at the yellow warning mark. He moved closer to the dial, positioning his head directly in line with the pointer to eliminate distortion. There was an almost imperceptible upward movement of the pointer.

"It's going higher. Townsend, how's that air sampler doing?" he called, without taking his eyes off the dials.

"It's normal, sir."

"This time it looks serious. We've got a leak from Number One reactor. There's a seepage somewhere from the chute that's caused the leak detector indicators to rise." He pulled off the heavy suit.

"What about using the dousing tank?" asked Townsend, his round face showing signs of strain.

The huge dousing tank high in the domed reactor building was for emergency use to dump millions of gallons of water on the reactor below. Johnson was against any rapid decision that would flood the station, despite the urgency for such a move. He rubbed his square chin thoughtfully. He mustn't do anything precipitously.

"The biggest danger is the possibility of contaminating the station ventilating system," he said calmly. "Get the handbook on it. It's one of the later volumes."

"Let's see," he said, very deliberately unfolding a large drawing from the back of the book. He spread it on the desk, holding down the folds with the corner of the telephone. "The chamber where the bundles are is here." He thrust a finger on an intersection of heavy lines on the drawing.

"The space is ventilated into the main vent system," he said. "If we closed down the reactor, the pressure would build up and contaminated air would flow into the ventilating system. Check on that air sampler again," he reminded Townsend.

"It's still normal, sir. I've instructed all station chemical staff to phone immediately if their fixed samplers show any change," Townsend reassured him.

Johnson swept his finger across the blueprint of the ventilation system, pausing at the point where the bundles were stuck in the chute.

"The suction effect is keeping fresh air in the chamber," he said slowly, half to himself. His mind was clear now: he knew that if he ran through the system logically he'd find a solution to the leak problem.

"If it didn't, radioactive air would contaminate the station," he continued.

"But we still have to get the bundles down the damaged chute and into the water tank," Townsend said.

Johnson ignored him. "I think the airflow is exactly balanced, but the only sure way is to measure it. We can't get right into the chamber—it's too hot, we've checked that." He stopped, as if deciding on a course of action. He glanced at Townsend. His voice had a ring of conviction.

"We could smash down the chute and the shielding and

cart it away with a mobile crane. We could get the vehicle into the chamber by tearing down this wall here—" He leaned over the drawing and traced a line with a finely sharpened pencil. "If we broke into this outside wall here the crane could enter at this point."

Townsend stared at the bold lines Johnson had drawn on the paper. He was a chemical engineer, used to formulas and symbols of another kind, and felt out of his depth looking at a structural blueprint.

"You're saying we should tear down the outside wall of the station?"

"Yes," Johnson replied coolly. "Take out the wall to get the crane in."

"What then? After you've broken down the wall?" Townsend exclaimed incredulously.

"Slice through the shielding and the chute with pneumatic drills and carry the whole lot away, bundles and all!"

"With the crane?"

"Yes—with the crane. A five-tonner should do it. There's enough maneuvering room in the chamber," Johnson said confidently. "Once we get the shielding with the bundles outside the building we can bury them."

"But how're you going to get the bundles out of the cracked-up shielding, sir?" Townsend asked. He still couldn't believe Johnson was seriously thinking of breaking down the wall.

"We don't! We'll leave them inside the shielding. Bury the whole thing—shielding, chute, and the two bundles!"

Johnson caught a glimpse of some of the technicians crowded around the outer perimeter of the control console, their faces tense as they stared at him.

"It's a drastic thing to do, but we're operating on borrowed time." He glanced at his watch. "I'm going to call Deighton and tell him." Just as he put out his hand to pick up the telephone the alarm klaxon burst into life and the red warning lights flashed.

Townsend, who'd had one eye on the air sampler, swung around and yelled: "The air-relief valve's blown! Pressure's rising in Number One reactor building!"

The men at the desk jumped. Johnson grabbed the desk microphone. The others crowded their action stations on the console.

"Attention! Attention! This is an emergency. Atmospheric pressure in Number One reactor building is above normal and rising. All personnel proceed to their emergency stations," he intoned.

He thrust the instrument into the shift controller's hand. "Repeat that every minute until you've said it ten times," he ordered.

He turned to Townsend. "Check all air pressures and station output. We're going to get rid of those bundles. I'll be in the service wing next to the chamber where they're stuck. Order the emergency team to meet me there." He paused and swept a hand over his face. "And get the maintenance department to bring a five-ton crane over to the service wing!"

The concrete outside wall of the chamber was tougher to break than Johnson had anticipated. Witzensky had ordered portable floodlights set up to shine on the wall, and two workmen using pneumatic drills cast gaunt shadows on the white face of the concrete, their bodies vibrating from the powerful equipment. Inside the chamber another pneumatic driller, dressed in a protective suit and headpiece, attacked the tough concrete of the shielding near the fissure at floor level. A relief buddy wearing a similar suit watched from some distance away.

EPICENTER

By 2:00 A.M. the outside party had outlined a hole about eighteen feet high and five feet wide in the exterior wall, which Johnson judged was not large enough to allow the crane to enter.

"We've got to drive the crane through here with the shielding in one complete piece. It'll have to be at least fifteen feet wide," he explained to Witzensky.

He thought a moment and then yelled: "First I'd better check with control on what's happening to the pressure in the reactor building."

He pressed a button on the portable radio transmitter-receiver inside a jeep he'd made into his outside headquarters for the demolition job. Townsend answered.

"Johnson here. What's the pressure in the reactor building?" he called, cupping his hand around the mouthpiece to shut out the din from the drills.

"Still rising. The air from the vent system must be sucking gobs of the radioactive stuff through the chamber down there."

Johnson switched off and looked at the drillers high on the scaffolding at the face of the curved concrete wall. They had penetrated the wall at the top and were steadily advancing downward along the two sides. By the time they had cut down to the ground a huge concrete slab would be ready to be divided into smaller chunks and pulled away, exposing the opening for the crane. Inside, the driller had completely severed the shielding and chute at floor level and had started on the portion that joined to the reactor-building wall.

Johnson walked to the wall, put his ear against the frigid surface, and heard the chattering drill of the man inside. He returned to the jeep. Something worried him. He ran over the sequence of moves in his mind. When the hole was completed in the outside wall the crane could enter, pick up the huge shielding complete with the severed chute and its cargo of fuel bundles, and retreat very slowly outside the building. The crane would then proceed a little way along the side of the station and carefully dump its radioactive load in a burial ground now being excavated by a bulldozer. The bulldozer would heap earth over the crumbling concrete, and when the radioactivity had eventually decayed to a point where it was safe to move the debris to a more permanent disposal ground, the mess would be moved away. It seemed in order.

The drillers on the outside face completed the cut down to the ground and were starting to drill horizontal and vertical lines to break the area into smaller squares which could be pulled away by the crane. Up in the control room Townsend watched the rising needles on the pressure gauges with growing concern. Abruptly their upward climb slowed and stopped.

"It must be the second relief valve opening," he said to the shift controller. "The pressure should steady now." He picked up the radio microphone and contacted the jeep outside.

"The pressure's stabilized now, sir," Townsend said loudly as the control room was flooded with the distant clatter of pneumatic drills.

"Okay," Johnson replied; then there was a click as he switched off.

The crane tore chunks of the heavy concrete from the wall. The rubble crashed to the frozen ground, churning the snow underneath into a bed of gray slush. Men ran clear as the crane advanced and retreated, its motor roaring, ejecting blue smoke from its vertical exhaust. Johnson looked at the devastation without emotion. It was part of a bigger plan to end the terrible predicament that faced the station operating staff. Watching the action relieved his tenseness.

The crane operator started to pull the concrete pieces from

the top of the outlined hole in accordance with Johnson's instructions and adjusted the swing of the chain to concentrate on the lower portion. Suddenly Johnson signaled to the foreman in charge to stop.

"You'll have to clear away this debris first. We've got to drive the crane into the building, so we'll need a clear path," he explained.

The foreman waved to the driver of the light bulldozer to approach. The man brought his vehicle into the floodlights' glare. It took four sweeps across the scene to pile the broken concrete pieces in a tidy heap on one side. The foreman gave the thumbs-up sign, the bulldozer retreated into the semidarkness, and the crane resumed operations. The wall crumbled faster as the hook grabbed with a better hold: pieces of concrete that broke off dragged other jagged slabs from the next layer down. Johnson could see the lights in the roof of the cavernous chamber, and the broken end of the shielding emerged through the rising dust. Only a few more minutes and the crane would be able to enter the chamber and pull the wretched shielding and its radioactive contents away, like taking some monstrous poisonous barb out of a wound.

A security guard appeared along the path that led from the gatehouse. He walked around the perimeter of the rubble and approached Johnson, cupping his hands to Johnson's ear.

"How many?" Johnson shouted above the racket.

"A whole crowd. They want to know what's up," the guard yelled.

Damn! Why hadn't he thought of the public? Word would have spread by now, even at this hour of the morning. The clangor from the crane and the crash of concrete must have awakened people. Johnson cursed himself for overlooking the public's reaction. A statement would be required. He passed a gloved hand over his cheek, now covered with a fine layer of concrete dust.

"Tell them we're making emergency repairs that couldn't wait until daytime," he instructed the man. "Say there's no danger, but it was something that had to be done immediately. Got it?"

The guard nodded and stomped through the snow toward the gatehouse. Johnson turned his attention to the crumbling wall. Only the bottom bit to go now. Most of the chamber was exposed to the floodlights, and he could see almost all of the shielding from the floor to where the severed end rested, like a drunk, against the inner wall of the reactor building.

The foreman ran up to Johnson. "I've got a sling ready to hoist the shielding when we get to it, sir. What about balance?" He struggled to make himself heard. "We don't want to tip it up."

"Spread the sling as wide as you can," Johnson yelled, moving his hands apart.

The man nodded. "Okay—I get it," he shouted, and strode, with the authoritative walk that foremen have when crossing construction sites, to a position where the crane operator could see him.

The roar from the engine quickly subsided, and he gave his instructions. The engine blurted and started again, and the crane put the finishing touches to its work of destruction. The bulldozer swung into action, ramming the broken pieces of concrete into mounds on each side of the opening. Johnson judged the hole to be high enough to swing the crane's load clear of the building. The bulldozer, its job done, rumbled away to make room for the crane to extricate itself from the hole after it had entered to pick up the shielding.

Two plastic-suited men carried a steel cable sling, which

had four cables with large snap hooks and rings so that they could be fastened around the shielding, and placed the central ring on the crane's hook. The foreman looked across at Johnson for the go-ahead signal. Johnson raised his hands high to hold everything, strode over to the jeep, and called Townsend on the radio.

"Pressure's stabilized, but it's still above normal, sir," Townsend said. "How're things going down there?"

"We're ready to move the crane in. Everything's all right so far. As soon as we get rid of the shielding and the bundles you can move in on the air pumps and auxiliaries."

Johnson put the instrument down. It was a cold night, but his hand glistened with sweat. Both the crane operator and the foreman had struggled into protective suits. He motioned to the foreman with an upheld hand, and the engine clattered and bellowed. The operator skillfully turned the crane and pointed it toward the opening. It moved forward slowly, the tip of the jib clearing the top of the hole with about a foot to spare. The sound of the engine suddenly became louder as it reverberated inside the chamber.

Johnson, the foreman, and a group of maintenance men followed the vehicle and stopped under the opening. The operator cautiously drove toward the shielding until the sling that swayed from the jib flicked the concrete, and then the two men in protective clothing deftly ducked under the shielding, grabbed the steel cables, connected the hooks, and spread the sling wide until the slack had gone out of it. When the foreman gave the thumbs-up sign to the operator the engine note changed to a whine as the operator applied upward tension on the crane hoist.

Nothing happened to the shielding. The whine changed to a growl, and slowly the huge assembly of concrete rose until it hung clear, dropping loose bits of concrete and dust from the raw ends of the shielding. It was coming away nicely—perfectly balanced, Johnson could see. The men had judged well when they positioned the sling. The shielding was edging clear of the hole in the reactor building wall and from the floor.

The operator backed the crane a foot, and carefully swung it sideways so that he could emerge from the building facing forward. Johnson waved the workmen away from the crane's path because anyone within fifty feet would be exposed to a dangerously high level of radioactivity. The men moved sluggishly, wanting to see the final stages of the drama. The foreman walked backward in front of the crane as it gingerly drove toward the outside wall.

The shielding assembly hung motionless from the sling as the operator carefully applied pressure on the throttle to get the vehicle over the rough threshold the drills had left, and the big rubber wheels rolled inexorably over the jagged edges. Johnson anxiously peered up at the jib. It cleared beautifully, and the shielding broke out under the full glare of the floodlights. The vehicle turned in the direction where the grave had been dug. Johnson was already at the jeep, radioing Townsend to find out what the pressure was now that the shielding had uncovered the hole in the reactor building wall.

"Same as it was. You've got it clear, then! What's that? What's happening—" Townsend yelled into the mouthpiece, then squeezed the instrument to his ear. The distant roar of the crane's engine suddenly stopped and he heard a thunderous crash, and men shouting and cries of alarm. From a far-off place he heard Johnson's voice roaring: "Run clear! It's splitting open!" The sounds fell away, and only the crackle of static spat from the speaker.

"What was that, sir?" a technician asked in a whisper.

"The shielding's cracked open! The bundles are exposed

completely!" Townsend said in an awed voice. He felt a blinding whiplash behind his eyes and the radio instrument fell from his hand.

The instrument buzzed. He recovered and picked it up. "Control. Townsend here," he snapped. Johnson was at the other end.

"Townsend—listen! The crane got the shielding out but tipped the bundles on the ground just outside the wall of the chamber. They're lying in the open air. The crane blew a tire. Check your air sampler immediately. I think radiation is being blown back into the chamber by the wind, getting through the hole in the reactor building and into the station ventilation system." He spoke rapidly.

"What's the recording on the air sampler?" Townsend yelled.

"Normal!" someone shouted.

"Atmosphere normal here," he called into the phone.

Johnson's voice was clear and precise: "Listen, Charlie! This is very important. Wait exactly one minute. That'll give it time to work its way through the system. If there's no change in one minute it'll be all right. After that keep a continuous check on it." He spoke again into the microphone. "Everybody's okay here. I'll hold on."

Townsend swiveled around so that he could watch the second hand on the clock. It was passing the quarter-hour mark. He peered at the air-sampler indicator. The needle was poised on normal, glued to the background dial. Fifteen seconds, twenty seconds . . . thirty-five seconds . . . the needle was as immobile as if it had been painted on. Forty-five . . . fifty-five . . . the needle was absolutely motionless. Fifty-eight . . . sixty . . . He sighed and moved the mouthpiece of the radiophone closer to his lips. The needle jerked upward, hovered momentarily, and climbed rapidly to the poison-contaminated air line. His eyes bulged. He reached out and touched the glass, as though trying to pull the needle back, staring at it in disbelief.

"Everybody out of the building!" he shouted, the instrument still raised to his lips. "The atmosphere's poisoned. Mr. Johnson, tell everybody down there to make for the main gatehouse. I'll meet you there in a few minutes. I'm going to shut down the station!" He slammed the microphone on its hook.

"Get out!" he shouted at the others.

They moved hesitantly toward the swinging doors. Townsend yelled again: "Get moving! Don't breathe this air!" He picked up the microphone on the desk.

"Attention! Attention everybody at Fairfield! Abandon the station! The ventilation system is contaminated. Everybody leave the station immediately. Repeat. Everybody is ordered to leave immediately. Immediately! Stop everything you are doing. We are shutting down the station. The air you breathe is poisoned!"

He made a swift movement to the console, pulled the reactor shut-off panel open, flicked off the main and auxiliary switches, checked that the reactor operation lights went out, and ran for the door.

SIX

Rita Johnson lay staring at the bedroom ceiling, studying the shadows cast by the light that filtered up from the street to her eleventh-floor apartment. The sound of a car on the nearby highway broke the silence, its studded tires biting into the mushy surface. She felt strange in the new apartment, and the droning of the car reassured her that other humans were awake at this early hour. She turned to look at the alarm clock on the night table. Three thirty. Hell, what an hour to wake up. It must be the reaction after Barbados. That, and the fact that she was sleeping on her own for the first time in four years. Imperceptibly, her mind wandered. She wondered if Ray also couldn't sleep. She tried to remember his schedule. Wasn't this the week he was on the nightshift, when they went through that refueling business or something?

She fluffed the pillow and put her cheek on the cool linen. It was no use. She swung out of bed, switched on the little bedside lamp, and lit a cigarette. The apartment was stuffy, overheated. She put on a frilly nightgown, opened the window a crack to let in the frosty air, and sat on the edge of the bed. In only a few hours she'd have to drive over to the buying office of Women's Wondawear Limited, where she worked. She'd be in no state to stomp the market, and Morris Weinstein no doubt would have a full slate of things he'd want done. That was why he paid her so well, wasn't it? As senior buyer it was her job to make sure the Women's Wondawear stores from coast to coast were stocked with garments that sold. A least she was nearer the buying office now that she lived in the northwest suburbs. It was only a ten-minute trip in her red Mustang.

She took another drag on the cigarette and stubbed it out. A dog barked in the distance, a frightened bark, then the night fell still. She straightened the bedclothes and slid her slender legs into the warmth between the sheets. The dog barked again, louder. Her eyelids fluttered momentarily, then closed.

Outside a new sound arose on the crisp night, slowly ascending in volume. The wailing of a siren, its resonance rising and then falling in an undulating tone. She stirred. Why does an ambulance have to make a racket at this hour? There's no traffic to fight. A second siren sounded, nearer, the two sounds in discord, one rising while the other fell. Another siren broke into a shrill note somewhere near. It sounded as if an ambulance or fire truck were approaching the building, and she suddenly went cold. She raised her head. Although the clamor grew louder, in some inexplicable way it was not coming nearer. A new noise joined the swelling cacophony, the bellow of a horn not far away. Rita jumped out of bed. A powerful siren shrieked nearby, so close it seemed to be inside the room. The blast soared up—up—up until it seemed it would never reach a peak; then it fell, the shock waves grabbing the bottom of her stomach. It quickly reversed and rose in a peal of reverberation that dinned her ears.

Rita spun into action. She ran to the window and savagely

pulled back the drapes. There was nothing on the street below, not even a parked car. The source of the nearest-sounding siren appeared to be over the rooftops of the houses farther down the road. That would put it somewhere in the direction of the avenue, where a few shops and some small office buildings were under construction.

A bedroom window lit up in the apartment block across the street, and the upper floor of the house on the corner suddenly blazed yellow. The undulating wails of the sirens continued, and each time the notes fell her stomach sank. One by one the lights in the apartment building opposite lit up, and silhouetted forms peered through the curtains. Then the light of a television screen glowed from the window directly opposite. She dashed to the set in the living room, switched it on, and knelt in front of it, hand on the tuning control. The screen lit up but no picture appeared. She flipped the knob from channel to channel. Nothing. She switched it off, ran into the bedroom, grabbed the transistor radio, and turned it on. Nothing but static. Irritated, she shoved the dial to another station. It yelped with a commercial for razor blades. She turned the knob slowly back to the first station, on the way passing a small triangle on the dial. A loud clear voice burst out and then went off. She reversed direction, steadied the pointer on the triangle. Funny, she'd never been able to get a station on that spot before.

". . . Emergency Measures Organization station Nacom Two now repeats its earlier message. A general emergency has been declared in the Metropolitan Toronto district as the result of a serious accident at the Fairfield Nuclear Power Station approximately twenty miles east of the downtown area. As a result, radioactive material has been discharged into the atmosphere and is being carried by a light easterly wind toward the city. As a safety precaution the director of EMO

74

has ordered the total evacuation of the city. Residents are requested to proceed with evacuation as quickly as possible. The complete facilities of EMO are operating. The regular police and auxiliary police will help guide you out of the city. Please obey their instructions. Residents in the Borough of North York should proceed north along the following routes: Highways 400, 11, and 27. Those living in the Borough of Scarborough should first head in a westerly direction. Signs directing traffic are already being placed in position. Residents in the Borough—"

She suddenly remembered a radio play her mother had told her about that took place before the war, something about Martians landing near New York—and everybody had panicked. But the racket outside—that was real. Besides, it wasn't likely they'd put on a play at nearly four o'clock in the morning. A feeling of unreality and disbelief swept over her oval face, and her muscles stiffened. There was a commotion outside in the corridor like the one last night when that second earthquake had slightly rocked the building. She went to the door and listened. Somebody yelled, "Better hurry or we'll all cop it." A door slammed, followed by the sound of someone rattling the lock for security. Footsteps hurried past, and then there were the voices of people congregating at the elevator. A baby cried. Car engines sounded on the street. She rushed to the window. It was true. People were running away. More than a dozen cars had already driven out of the underground parking lot, and more emerged even as she watched, their exhausts steaming in the cold air.

She switched on the radio. ". . . and reception centers are now being set up in Barrie, about 60 miles north of Toronto; Orillia, a few miles north of Lake Simcoe; Shelbourne, about 50 miles northwest; Peterborough, 80 miles northeast; and in Bracebridge. Obey the special disaster directional signs and you will be able to drive out of the city with the least trouble. Keep to the speed limit. Do not hurry. Take with you any emergency pack you may have already prepared. This should contain enough food to last one adult for seven days . . ." Her blue eyes opened wide. "Seven days!"

". . . should include two gallons of drinking water or as much as can be carried. Canned fruit juices, soups, corned beef, and canned vegetables should also be included. For each child up to three years include four large cans of evaporated milk and three gallons of water. A first-aid kit consisting of . . ."

Her mouth dropped open. Enough for seven days! That's ridiculous. She fingered her fine light hair, indecision etched in little worry lines around her mouth. If Ray were here he'd know what to do. It was making the decision to go or not that was difficult. She never liked running with the crowd; her sense of independence was strong. If she had to decide on buying coats or women's dresses she could rely on her instinct, make a snap decision, and be right ninety-nine per cent of the time. At twenty-nine Rita Johnson had built up a name for herself in the business world. She'd been with Woman's Wondawear for eight years, and progressed from stockroom clerk to her present position by a superabundance of energy and a persuasive personality. Her uncanny talent for buying had saved the company hundreds of thousands of dollars since her transfer to the buying department six years ago. Down on the "Avenue," as the garment manufacturers' famous Spadina Avenue was known in the trade, they called her Rita Right. Buyers from rival firms asked "What's Rita looking at this season?" before committing themselves.

She heard tires whine on the frozen street below as drivers gunned their engines. The sirens, which had subsided, suddenly started to wail again. She felt alone. Damn those hellish things! She went into the bathroom, washed her face in cold water, and started to dress. A car horn blew impatiently. It'll be murder on the highways. Perhaps she could find some backroads that ran parallel to the main highway north, but with her sense of direction she'd be lost. She'd have to stick to the highway and take a chance.

The two flight bags she'd taken to Barbados were on the floor where she'd thrown them after unpacking. She quickly took out the odds and ends she hadn't emptied, put in some cans of food from the refrigerator, two cans of noncaloric ginger ale, and packed both bags with three changes of outer clothes, layers of lacy black underwear, and a shimmering gold evening dress, all with the exclusive Women's Wondawear label. She spent so much time carefully folding her clothes that she forgot to put in a can opener. She finally slung a fur cape over her shoulders—a special bonus from Morris Weinstein—and went out into the deserted corridor.

Thankfully the car started without trouble. She drove up the ramp and passed a line of cars parked in front. People were loading the trunks with picnic hampers and cartons. She was surprised that it took only a few minutes to drive to Highway 400, the main road to Barrie. Being so near the north end of the city gave her a head start on the mass of cars that at that moment was fighting to get out of the downtown area.

She lit a cigarette, turned on the radio, and fiddled with the knob until she found the right spot on the dial.

". . . and the Emergency Measures Organization repeats the official announcement regarding the order to evacuate Toronto . . ."

The announcer read the earlier text. When he came to the end he added: "A new item has just been handed to me. Due to an accident at the corner of Highway 11 and Steeles Avenue, a detour has been ordered for all traffic proceeding north up Yonge Street. At Finch Avenue proceed west to Bathurst Street and continue north before cutting back to Highway 11. I'll repeat the instruction . . ."

Rita opened the glove compartment and searched for a map among the old gasoline credit card chits, the car's service handbook, and some dress manufacturer's mail catalogue. The map wasn't there. She glanced at the speedometer. Nearly fifty. If she kept up this speed she'd be at one of the reception centers in well under two hours, making allowances for a traffic jam at Barrie or maybe getting around some accident scene.

". . . to obey police instructions at all times. Canadian Armed Forces personnel have been called in to help the police maintain an orderly evacuation of the city. These personnel, mainly soldiers, must also be obeyed. The director of EMO reminds drivers and passengers that military personnel are authorized as peace officers and have the power of arrest. Follow the route signs you will find posted at main intersections. Owners of summer cottages should make for them; others should follow the signs posted 'Reception Center,' which will appear at cutoffs on the main northerly routes beginning approximately forty miles north of the city. The EMO is setting up these reception centers for people needing basic shelter: village schools, public buildings, and church halls. Portable buildings are being set up near the small towns and villages north of this forty-mile zone. Although these buildings will be heated, everybody is advised to dress warmly and take along a supply of sweaters and extra headgear . . ."

The cape settled around her shoulders, giving a warm, snug feeling. Suddenly the brake lights of the car ahead glowed red, then went out. She glanced in the rear-view mirror. That guy behind was too close. Rita leaned forward and put on her parking lights. It was an old trick she'd discovered to warn tailgaters, who, for some reason, always seemed to pick on woman drivers—at least that was her experience. To the driver behind, the rear lights appeared to be the brake lights flashing on, and this one took the hint and slowed down.

She smiled and lit another cigarette, rolling down the window slightly to clear the smoke. The traffic sped up. She listened to the radio again.

". . . and special trains have been directed into Union Station for people without their own means of transportation. Gray Coach Lines, Greyhound buses, and other coaches are being assembled at the central bus terminal at Bay and Dundas Streets. Other buses of the Toronto Transit Commission will leave all subway stations. The subway trains are now beginning to run. Take any bus. They will all travel to a northern point and stop at the special reception areas now being set up. Oh—one moment, please. Here is the latest communiqué from the regional director of the EMO. The radioactive discharge that resulted from an accident to the Fairfield Nuclear Station about twenty miles"—she leaned forward and turned up the volume—"east of Toronto is reported to be moving on a freshening easterly wind toward the heart of the downtown district. The Department of Transport weather office calculates that the first edge of the discharge will arrive near the City Hall in about forty-five minutes. It is therefore vitally important that the center of the downtown area be evacuated at once. Everybody in an area bounded by a line from the waterfront—including the Toronto Islands—and north to St. Clair Avenue must proceed at once . . ."

My God! She was lucky. The poor devils downtown. And Ray? He'd be heading north like everyone else. Surely the station would be the first place they'd evacuate; it was the center of the danger zone, the cause of the whole mess. He knew how to take care of himself. But his bloody sense of devotion to duty, that stubborn streak. Little signals of doubt flew up at the back of her mind.

"Idiot!"

Rita swerved to avoid the ambulance that shot out of the country schoolhouse yard five miles north of Barrie.

She uttered the word more in relief than anger. The lonely drive north had taken longer than she'd estimated. She had come across a line of stalled cars at one point, held up by a big transport truck that had run out of fuel in the middle of the highway. A grisly three-car pile-up just south of Barrie had further delayed her. Now, as the sun began to light up the snow-laden fields on each side of the narrow country road and the late-winter birds fluttered over the bare trees, the reality of the moment seemed like a dream. Her throat was parched. Chain-smoking two packs of cigarettes hadn't helped, and her mouth felt furry as she ran her tongue around the inside of her teeth.

She braked the car outside the schoolhouse and read the words on the board nailed to a wooden rail: EMO Reception Center No. 5. The half-acre yard was choked with official vehicles—stake trucks, a row of trucks converted into ambulances, and, at the far end, a rank of large covered trucks with grim signs painted on the tailboards: Dead Disposal—EMO Southern Ontario Region.

She shuddered and her mouth tightened, but not from fear. Anything that reminded Rita of death depressed rather than frightened her; she had determined years ago—since she left high school—that she would never think of three things: death, growing fat, or becoming old and wrinkled. She had successfully kept her resolution. She thought no moribund thoughts, looked after her youthfully slim body carefully, and never dwelt on the question of time. After her twenty-first birthday she refused to acknowledge natal anniversaries, but she lately had got into the habit of running her fingers over the silky skin of her hips when she stepped out of the shower before posing nude in front of the full-length mirror in her bathroom, turning this way and that to check her figure with a critical eye.

She found a crumpled cigarette package in the glove compartment and lit the last cigarette. She turned down the window, blew out the smoke, and inhaled the country air, sweet and chilly. It smelled clean, and she tossed the cigarette into the snowbank at the side of the road, where it sizzled and died.

She'd met Ray at a New Year's Eve party someone had dragged him to, and had been fascinated by his tall refined appearance and quiet charm, so different from the slick men she associated with in her daily round of showrooms and business offices. She had liked his straight black hair and immaculate grooming and had suddenly found herself thinking what she could change about him to mold him into the perfect man. Ray had been whisked off his feet by this scintillating whirlwind of a woman who took such a vital interest in him. He had never considered himself particularly good-looking, but Rita made him feel as though he were the handsomest and most important man in the world: which Raymond Johnson, nuclear expert, was—to her.

They had been married shortly afterward and had taken an apartment in downtown Toronto. He worked at the Fairfield power station, while Rita continued in her job with Women's Wondawear.

She had glowed with a quiet pride at the respect paid to him by his small circle of friends, the nuclear engineers and physicists from the station, several of whom had been at university with him. They knew his background: his brilliant mind, his ability to strike at the heart of an engineering problem, his graduation with top honors. It had come as no surprise to them when, after his station-operating course, he quickly rose from shift controller to executive chief engineer at Fairfield, the youngest ever to be appointed to the position.

A man dressed in a creased uniform with a broad red EMO armband came running out of the front door of the schoolhouse. He called out, "You can't drive in here, miss. It's reserved for officials. You'll have to park over there."

He pointed across the road to a parking sign that she hadn't noticed. A few private cars were already drawn up in a field, from which the top layer of loose snow had been swept clear. It was obvious that she had arrived ahead of the crowd, and she parked the car where the officious man had indicated.

"You're one of the early birds, miss," the man said, his eyes lingering on her nylons as she swung her legs out of the car and pulled on fur-trimmed snowboots.

"Where do I go from here?"

"From here? This is it, miss. You must stay here until the all-clear sounds and you can go back to the city."

"When will that be?" she demanded, leaning back to check her hair in the rear-view mirror.

The man shrugged. "Who knows? Coupla days I s'pose," he said vaguely.

Rita frowned. When men spoke in vague terms they were usually trying to protect a woman's sensitivity. It angered her. She didn't want to be protected by any man; she was capable of taking care of herself. In her profession she had to. Temptation was her constant companion: bribery had been practiced in the seller-buyer relationship since the dawn of history. For a male buyer the traditional methods of corruption— beautiful women, backhanded money deals (always cash, of

course), vacations in plush Florida apartments with everything laid on—were common enough in certain manufactur-
ing houses. For a woman buyer the stakes often assumed more
tangible forms—women were so complicated—mink coats,
new cars with power this and power that, and, at one time,
Rita had been offered a free two-year lease on a luxury apartment in the best part of town, with furniture of her choice.

She got out of the car and walked to the schoolhouse. Inside the entrance a woman and three children were being
asked to fill out a form by a girl who sat behind a long trestle
table. Through the open swinging doors behind, Rita could
see workers erecting two-tier wooden bunk beds, and the
sound of hammering echoed in the hall. She puckered her lips,
picked up one of the forms, and idly looked at it, waiting for
the woman ahead to move on.

She had never accepted any of the attractive offers in the
buying racket, but that didn't mean she hadn't had her share
of fun. She liked parties and mixing with people; anything
that smacked of officialdom, like the form she now held in
her delicately gloved hand, was anathema. She was never
short of company—male company—at the parties she attended after the new season's buying had been completed at
some manufacturer's showroom, but she had never betrayed
Ray. Never, that is, until that buying trip in Rome two years
ago.

The stage had been set long before she went to Rome.
After two years of marriage she had concluded that she and
Ray would hardly be able to make a go of it: their natures
and living habits were as disparate as those of an eager, lively
young mare and a young but handsome Clydesdale champion.

Ray's life had gone through a traumatic upheaval. He'd
traded his quiet rooming-house domesticity for a one-bed-
room apartment with a female companion who could never

sit still for one evening. Rita had come home an hour later than he did when he was on the day shift, and Ray cooked the evening meal, which he hadn't minded doing. But after dinner Rita would want to get out and see the town, go to a night-club or a party, or sometimes even drive to Niagara Falls, ninety miles away, for a cocktail in the Rainbow Room of the Sheraton-Brock Hotel overlooking the floodlit cascade.

"Shall I put all their names in this little space?" the woman asked, indicating her three children with a sweep of her arm.

"Yes, with their Christian names and middle names. They *do* have middle names, don't they?" the girl asked, implying that it was sinful for children not to be blessed with middle names.

Inevitably their marriage had run along predictable lines. She wouldn't come home until the early hours, after staying on at a sales party or joined a theater group downtown. Ray, content to relax with an engineering journal, accepted her absence philosophically. When he was on the refueling night shift he rarely saw her except when she came home earlier than usual.

"See you," was his formula good-by before he took the elevator to the garage and got into his car for the three-mile drive to Fairfield. They rarely engaged in sex, which at one time had acted as a salve for their bruised personalities; in recent months this activity had almost ceased.

"Oh—you didn't fill in their ages," the girl behind the table said sternly as a group of people came through the door. "You'll have to put that down in this space."

Rita took a deep breath and looked at the newcomers, two families who knew each other, with five young children who were half asleep. The husbands carried traveling cases that bulged with personal belongings, and one woman struggled with a huge valise. Rita pressed close to the table and said impatiently, "Do I have to fill in one of these?"

The girl's eyes opened wide. "Of course. Everybody's got to register. It's the regulation."

"But I'm alone. I haven't got—I don't have any children."

"Everybody's got to," an EMO man standing in the background exclaimed.

She put her handbag on the table and fished for a pencil.

"It's got to be in ink," said the girl, eyeing the pencil.

"I don't have a pen."

"Then you'll have to wait until the ballpoint's free."

Rita stamped her heel on the floor and strove to keep her temper under control. One of the men who had just come in said, "Here, use mine."

"Thanks," she said slowly, and took the pen.

She poised the ballpoint over the paper and suddenly heard Greg's voice say, "Here, use mine." She'd looked around for a pen to register at the Rome hotel and he'd offered his. She knew enough about men to know an approach when she saw one. She had dismissed him from her mind when she'd finished with the pen and handed it back with a polite thank you. She didn't see him for the rest of the four-day buying trip, until the last day, when she found herself back at the hotel about one o'clock in the afternoon with the rest of the day free. She had made her decisions at the fashion houses and was faced with the prospect of putting her paperwork in order before stealing a sightseeing trip around the city after lunch. The girl at the front desk suggested the open-air roof restaurant. "It is a beautiful view, signora, and the rush is over," she added, looking at her watch.

The restaurant was nearly empty. Waiters were cleaning off the tables and flicking crumbs from the wicker seats with serviettes. They deftly removed the soiled tablecloths and replaced them with fresh linen.

Rita looked out over the rooftops. In the middle distance the archways of the Colosseum were sharply outlined against the sky, and partially restored ruins of Corinthian columns and ancient statuary lay about in newly excavated sites in nearby streets. The sounds of Rome filtered up to her, the snarl of little Fiats and buzzing motor scooters and the occasional shout of an excited citizen. She sipped an *apéritif*, enjoying the early-summer sunshine. After the hectic days of being keyed up, her body and mind began to relax. She was soon the only one in the little restaurant; the few preseason tourists had melted away. She heard the elevator doors close behind her and was faintly aware of footsteps approaching.

"Hullo there—enjoying Rome?"

It was he. He stood near her table, but not close enough to suggest that she ought to ask him to join her. He held a folded American newspaper in his hand.

"Hi. It's a beautiful city."

"First time?" He smiled, and she noted the pleasant curve of his mouth and the rather full nose, almost ugly.

"How'd you guess?" she laughed. "This is the first time I've had a chance to look at it." She indicated the city below with a nod of her head.

"Shot in the dark," he replied. "You American?"

"No, Canadian."

"Ah—I was in Montreal once. Swinging city. But you're probably from Toronto?"

"Amazing. Do you do this for a living?"

"Right first time. I fly with the jet set and when they bore me I'm an international racketeer playing the tables on transatlantic liners. I can guess where anybody comes from just by looking at them," he laughed, more at her than with her. She could see that he wasn't hurt.

"Care to tell me all about your nefarious life?" she found herself saying, indicating a chair. Months later, when she thought about that moment, she wondered if she had said it merely to make up for her unkind remark.

He was a salesman for a Chicago toy manufacturer on a one-man sales mission to various European countries. He'd been in Italy a week, having come in from Milan the day he met her at the registration desk.

At midnight she found herself in one of those intimate bars that flourish around the Via Veneto, dancing to the soft tones of a five-piece band of smiling musicians and feeling warm and secure in his arms. They had earlier sauntered up the Spanish Steps, and had a drink or two sitting at a sidewalk table outside Doney's watching the smartly dressed Romans promenading and flirting at nearby tables. There were few people in the bar, and the violinist strolled from the band platform and followed them around the floor.

When they got back to the hotel it was almost two o'clock. They both complained about aching feet.

"And I don't even have a bath in my room, just a shower," Greg said. It was a trial balloon. "So come and dip your feet in mine." Ray, Women's Wondawear, and Toronto were a million miles away.

In the bedroom she smiled at his simulated Italian tenor as he scrubbed in the bath. He suddenly stopped and said something. "What's that?" she called.

"I said, my back needs scrubbing. It's an old Italian custom."

"Liar!"

"It is—really. Especially in the country districts."

EPICENTER

"This is Rome."

"So do as the Romans do!"

"All right, Roman, but make sure your toga's on!" She laughed.

He was sitting in the bath, holding out a soaped washcloth. She rolled up her sleeve and ran the cloth in circles over his back. He uttered a deep sigh of contentment. Suddenly their heads were together and he was kissing her. He grasped her around the neck with wet hands.

"You're ruining my hairdo." She broke way. "And look at my dress! It's all wet."

"So take it off—and join me!"

Without replying, she rinsed her hands in the basin to remove the soap and dried them on a towel. Then she went into the bedroom, took off her dress, slip, panties, bra, and stockings, and went back into the bathroom . . .

"Thank you." She handed the pen to the young husband. "Good job you brought your own. Talk about organization! They expect crowds of people and provide one pen—" Her eyes were distant.

"You're next," the girl said curtly. She studied the form Rita had filled in, grunted to show she had filled in everything that was necessary, and said, "Take Bunk C.5. You can put your personal possessions in the locker underneath. Here's the key."

The odd bunk numbers were on the upper tier. Rita went back to the car and struggled across the road with the two flight bags. The improvised parking lot was almost filled up, and people were streaming into the old schoolhouse. They reminded her of refugees from a war movie: she shuddered and thought of other things, particularly of how to hang her dresses in a locker only two feet high built under the lower berth.

EPICENTER

The schoolhouse had an assembly hall and two classrooms. Women and children were allocated the hall and the men the two smaller rooms, the children staying with their mothers. There was a kitchen leading off the hall and women from the village were making hot drinks and trying to organize the food supplies that had been sent in. The schoolhouse was under the supervision of an EMO official, a tall fatherly-looking man who had a small staff of men under him.

Rita went to the window at the end of the hall and looked out. At the back of the school, hidden from the road, was a barn. The fence between the schoolyard and the barn had been torn down and wooden planks laid in a rough roadway. Over the big entrance someone had nailed a sign—EMO Medical Ward 1—and workmen were unloading bunk beds from a big truck drawn up outside, stamping their feet to keep warm. She looked away and returned to the bunk, laid out her clothes on the rough mattress, and realized she couldn't store all her things in the locker. She took one of the flight bags to the car, locked it inside, and went back to the assembly hall.

A dumpy woman was standing at her bunk looking at the number on it and comparing it with the number on the pink form the registration girl had given her. A tall willowy girl of about fourteen had her arm about the woman's waist.

"Hi there. Are you in the lower berth?" Rita asked the woman, who turned and looked at her with pale dull eyes. The girl looked up, and Rita noted the fair skin and the delicate light brown hair under the hat. She'd look gorgeous in that teen-age spring number Rita had bought in Montreal, especially if she wore her hair combed down over her forehead. She studied the girl's face.

"That's right. You in the top berth?" The woman's voice was tired.

Rita nodded. The kid was pretty enough to be a model. She

could see her in a creation by Petite Modes du Montreal, one of the fashion houses she bought from.

"Like being on a ship," the woman continued. "My name's Rosie—Rosie Long, and this is Shirley."

The girl smiled, a brief crinkling of the nose and a flickering around the mouth.

"Did you have much trouble getting here?" Rosie Long asked.

"No—I was early, beat the rush. You?"

Rosie Long didn't reply immediately, and Rita had the feeling she had asked something embarrassing.

"No—no. We came on the bus." She busied herself unlocking the suitcase she'd brought and looked at the wooden locker built under the lower bunk.

"I guess we can start unpacking, Shirley," she said, turning to the girl. She took the few clothes out of the case and laid them on the rough wooden shelf in the locker, along with a few cans of vegetable soup and some canned meat.

Rita watched the girl help her mother straighten the clothes. There was something about her that she couldn't quite figure out. Rita was a pretty good judge of people—in her job she had to be. Something nagged at her mind, but she couldn't define it. Suddenly she heard herself say, "I can take the bunk across the way and you and Shirley will have the same piece of furniture, Rosie."

"That's very kind of you," Rosie Long replied, "but it'll be okay this way. Like this Shirley'll be right across the aisle from me, where I can keep an eye on her—"

She stopped, and looked away. Shirley, closely watching her mother's face as she spoke, seemed to withdraw. She sat on her bunk and opened a comic book.

"I wonder how long we're supposed to stay here," Rita said, changing the subject.

EPICENTER

"I dunno. 'Ope it's not for long. I had to leave in such a hurry I'm almost sure I left all the lights on. Oh look, here's somebody else coming in this row."

She nodded toward a husband and wife with three young children who had stopped at a bunk farther along the aisle. The father slung a big leather suitcase on the lower bunk and then hurriedly put a carrying bag on three other beds to make sure people could see they were taken. He disappeared and returned with a huge red Coke cooler, which he heaved on the bare wooden floor with a metallic thud.

"Looks like they're checking in for the season!" Rita whispered in a confidential tone to Rosie Long, who tittered politely, sharing some vague feeling of communion with the attractive young woman.

The first morning people were occupied with trying to settle down in the unfamiliar and uncomfortable surroundings. Many tried to catch up on much-needed sleep. By midafternoon the adults had partially recovered and lined up before the long trestle table that workmen had erected near the kitchen, where the women from the village had set out dishes of hot soup, sandwiches, coffee, and milk for the children. They quickly organized a baby-bottle-warming service for the mothers and even had a diaper disposal and renewal system going, and fresh linen was brought in from an EMO Medical Supply truck parked in the schoolyard.

Toward evening, Rita tried to drive her car out of the rough parking lot, but it was hemmed in by late-arriving vehicles. She decided to walk the quarter mile to the other side of the village, where she'd heard there was a restaurant and cinema, and had walked about thirty yards when an EMO truck came up behind her and stopped. A farm boy rolled down the window.

"Wanna lift, miss?" he called expectantly.

She climbed up beside him. "I'm Jim. Bit of a to-do back there." He stared at her short skirt, then tossed his head in a southerly direction which Rita took to mean Toronto.

"Yeah. Heard how long it's going to be before we can go back?" She clutched the rusting side of the cab as the truck bounced over the rutted road covered with frozen muck churned up by the tires of hundreds of cars.

"An EMO guy told me it would be at least a week, maybe more. They're scared about the wind changing now. 'Ow far yer goin'?"

"Just to the village. Somebody told me there's a restaurant there."

The farm boy laughed and scratched his untidy hair.

"Why—isn't there?"

"There used to be—till this morning."

"What do you mean?"

"Elmer Belwood ran a cafe until the EMO guys took 'im over this mornin', when the 'mergency 'appened."

He slowed down at the junction of the main street through the village, moved the gear shift deftly, and let his eyes run over her legs.

"The EMO took all Elmer's stock early this mornin'. 'E's 'ad to close 'is place down," the boy continued. "Where'd yer like me to drop yer off, miss? 'Ere's the village main street."

"Right here. Thanks for the ride," she said.

The street consisted of half a dozen stores, some cottage-type wooden houses fronting on it on either side, and a small bank; the cinema turned out to be a sleazy beer parlor with pinball machines and a room at the back where old movies were shown every Thursday night.

Rita walked down the street in the half light. There were only a few people about, and those she passed turned and stared—it wasn't often they saw a well-dressed woman in city clothes walking through the village. She suddenly felt alone and depressed, among unfriendly people, and thought of Ray. She vaguely missed his quiet confidence and taciturn nature. Despite his diffidence, there had always been something reassuring about his presence, a kind of stability, even if he was stuffy at times.

She turned and started back to the reception center. It was now dark, and she could see through the uncurtained windows of the small houses that some of the evacuees were being housed by individual families. The EMO, through its government sources, was paying a small billeting allowance to private householders for this service. Rita wondered how the city people would get on with the locals, and was undecided whether she would have preferred to be in a house rather than take her chances with less parochial people in the center. The center was depressing enough, but to be stuck in one of these horrible pokey houses—she made an ugly movement with her mouth, pulled up her collar, and walked on.

At the center a long line of cars was drawn up on the side road, the queue extending to the schoolhouse. The latecomers were arguing with two EMO officials at the door. A telephone line had been hastily run into the front entrance of the school and an official was frantically calling other centers around Barrie and farther afield to see if space could be found for the new arrivals. He did his job well: he located an almost empty center someone had forgotten about near the small town of Orillia, about twenty miles to the north. He gave directions to the drivers, and they turned around in the schoolyard and edged down the road to the highway two miles away.

Rita went indoors and an official asked her for her slip of

paper before he'd let her enter the assembly hall. The lights had been dimmed, and small groups of husbands and wives stood near the table outside the kitchen drinking coffee and talking in hushed voices. The younger children had been put to bed, and here and there an older child was helping her mother arrange clothing and other personal possessions.

At the corner near her bunk Rita saw Rosie Long sitting on the edge of the bed, her head bent, with closed eyes. Her daughter was on the other side, dressed in pretty pink pajamas, kneeling on the bare boards, her hands together in prayer. Rita watched silently as the girl's mouth moved, and she strained to hear the words Shirley formed so deliberately with her lips, but there was no sound; not even a lisp escaped her. In a flash Rita realized that the girl was a deaf-mute.

SEVEN

As the predawn light brightened the eastern sky a Sikorsky CH-53 helicopter swooped over the town of Aurora a few miles north of Toronto. It hovered momentarily, then settled behind the leafless trees a hundred yards down a side road.

The rotor free-wheeled for a few minutes, and before it stopped a small group of men climbed out, their heads bent. They walked past another CH-53 parked on the snow-covered landing space and hurried to an opening in an earth-and-sandbagged mound.

Before he stepped in the doorway, Johnson glanced back at Townsend. There were other men behind him, either dressed in uniform or wearing official armbands, and one of the two pilots was also crossing to the opening.

To motorists who flashed past on the highway the snow-covered mound looked like a half-completed basement of a large house. A residence for a nonconformist perhaps, or for someone who shunned the sterile new housing developments that had sprung up during recent years around the fringes of the small towns and villages north of Toronto. The lush farming land had been rapidly gobbled up by housing developers who paid the long-established farmers high prices. Prevented from expanding south because of Lake Ontario, Toronto had spread sideways and upward like a fat cat. New residential areas sprang up east, west, and north, especially north, between the city limits and the resort area on the southern shore of Lake Simcoe about fifty miles away. Torontonians escaped to the lake to avoid the summer heat, and in winter the more hardy fished through holes in the ice.

North is where the action is, the real estate salesmen said glibly, viewing the straggly lines of new houses in the tree-less subdivisions that had cropped up near Thornhill, Richmond Hill, and Aurora, little communities that had once lain undisturbed on the crests of the rolling upland slopes. The bulldozers clattered and rammed the earth, preparing the way for the concrete pourers, the bricklayers, the carpenters and roofers.

The air was warm and heavy when Johnson lowered his head to duck under the doorway leading down the steps to the subterranean operations center of the Metropolitan Toronto Department of Emergency Services. The heavily reinforced steel-and-concrete building was the control center for evacuation and rescue operations in case of a direct nuclear attack or a peacetime disaster. It was connected with three subsector centers a few miles east, west, and north that were similarly equipped with radio, telephone, and data-code communications to the federal EMO headquarters in Ottawa. The lines of communication were spread in an invisible network of intelligence to regional headquarters in each of the other nine provincial capitals and were also connected with United States centers.

The centers were manned twenty-four hours a day, seven days a week, every month of the year, by key officials and workers who lived at two levels in a semifantasy world. One was the "real" world of streets, houses, automobiles, movies, family quarrels, love affairs, and monthly household budgets; the other world was of underground bunkers, buried headquarter buildings, often silent telephone switchboards, deserted conference rooms, and lonely hours studying wall maps and disaster-procedure techniques. The luckier ones were selected to take special courses at the Emergency Measures College at Arnprior, near Ottawa, where they met new faces and updated their knowledge of civil defense.

Emergency legislation giving officials power to operate in case of attack had long ago been drafted and included in the Government War Book, a thick tome buried in a vault that was easily accessible to the Cabinet Room in Ottawa. There was a popular joke among some middle-power permanent civil servants on Parliament Hill that if war broke out the Prime Minister would have to do two things before he could act: pick up the red telephone and speak to the President of the United States, and call him again after he'd consulted the Government War Book. Presumed anomalies in the book were the butt of senior officials' humor, but EMO had conscientiously tried to iron out the conflicting responsibilities of the federal and provincial governments. In case of an attack, the Prime Minister had only to invoke the War Measures Act to give the federal government overall control of all provincial and municipal governments.

Johnson glanced at Townsend's face in the brightly lit room at the bottom of the steps. His features were drawn tight, his forehead deeply etched.

"This way, gentlemen."

The little group of visitors turned to face a tall, thin man who stood near the inner door. Although he was dressed in civilian clothes, he had a military look about him. His penetrating hazel eyes swung easily across the knot of men before him, registering each detail. He had a long nose and a precisely clipped bristly moustache that partly covered a thin upper lip. He's pretty high up, Johnson thought, possibly Department of National Defense. Johnson, nearest the door, stepped into a moderately sized room with a long table surrounded by comfortable-looking chairs, about half of which were already occupied by men, some in uniform.

The man with the authoritative bearing hurried to the head of the table. "I'm Ferrisston—EMO director," he said tersely, and proceeded to make rapid introductions around the table. "Forget the handshakes," he added curtly, as several men rose and stretched their hands toward the newcomers. "Let's get cracking!"

Ferrisston's voice was sharply incisive, with an overtone of officiousness. He still wore the short topcoat he'd hurriedly put on when the first signal came through on the evacuation. He took some papers from a folder on the table—transcripts of radio messages flashed to the Aurora base—and put on oversized horn-rimmed glasses.

"Evacuation of Metro Toronto is still proceeding. There've been some tie-ups and bottlenecks which we hadn't anticipated, but on the whole the situation is under control," he said, moving his scraggy hands for emphasis.

Johnson glanced across the table at two officials from Ottawa who had been with him in the helicopter. They had been picked up at Toronto International Airport after the Fairfield group had been flown there from the abandoned power station. From the Federal Department of Health and Welfare, they were responsible for supervising setting up casualty-clearing centers and feeding stations and for establishing the mobile hospitals which Ottawa had located in major cities across the country. They showed no emotion as Ferrisston labored on. Johnson suddenly realized he'd made an error in evaluating Ferrisston: the piercing eyes and brusque manner concealed a feeling of inadequacy, a lack of confidence. But on the whole the situation is under control! Johnson bit his lower lip hard to keep his feelings in check. Where had everybody been looking when the helicopter had gone from the airport in the western suburbs to the Aurora base in the north? The aircraft had flown low, to stay below stray plumes of radioactive air that had dispersed from Fairfield. As the helicopter had sped across the broad Highway 401—the Toronto bypass—Johnson had seen the bright headlights of thousands of stationary cars extending eastward for miles, and red rear lights stretching westward. The twelve-lane highway had been a river of stalled cars. Dozens of tributaries poured cars toward the blocked main stream, backing up into the side streets where the matchbox surburban houses stood, some lit, most in darkness.

The pilot had held course directly above Highway 11, knowing that it would take him directly to Aurora. Mysteriously, there had been a gap in the traffic from the Thornhill intersection until the cutoff for Ottawa. There the traffic had crept forward. Along the highway there had been a double line of unmoving cars, with one line detouring through a field. Johnson had seen the reason for the detour: a huge tractor-trailer sprawled like a wounded dinosaur across the highway, completely stopping traffic in both directions.

In downtown Toronto there was even worse confusion. As always when disaster strikes, the poor were hit hardest. Many who had no cars had to depend on public transportation to take them out of the core of the city. They streamed in family groups, laden with hand luggage and shopping bags, toward the intersection of Yonge and Queen Streets, Toronto's traditional shopping center, a conglomeration of drab, ugly retail stores and banks made over with facing tile and embossed store names in a halfhearted and economical attempt at modernization. Yonge Street was a north-south thoroughfare that started near the lake and shot north like an unwavering arrow, and was the east-west dividing line for the city. A stream of maroon streetcars hastily dispatched by the Transit Commission when EMO had alerted them, was stalled on the west side of Queen Street. They were headed the wrong way, toward the east—the very direction people were fleeing from. A policeman at the side of the road operated the traffic signals from a control box he'd opened with his key. He favored the northbound traffic, and this caused the westbound cars to clog the street. Horns sounded impatiently and anxious faces peered out of windows, looking at the eastern sky.

People poured down the subway entrance to the underground trains under the stern eyes of two soldiers armed with stubby automatic rifles. Nearby a young officer held a walkie-talkie to his mouth. A throng of people pushing along the narrow sidewalk thrust forward to get around a woman who half knelt by a baby carriage with a broken front wheel, full of bulky packages that were shoved in around the child. The woman shrieked; "Don't step on my baby!" The people behind pushed forward, sending the woman in a sprawling heap across the baby.

A young man, white-eyed with fear, trampled over her, followed by a man carrying a huge cabin trunk, who tripped and fell. The trunk hinges snapped, spilling soiled clothing, bolts of new cloth and phonograph records. Others piled into the man and the trunk, falling against the rising heap of humanity that struggled and squirmed, yelling and shouting, hemmed in by the buildings on one side and the cars near the curb. The policeman continued to operate his control switch, unaware of the crowd suffocating less than forty yards away.

One of the soldiers looked up, saw the turmoil, and nudged his companion, who alerted the officer. The officer snapped an order and nodded for a soldier to accompany him. They were good soldiers. They had been trained never, never to break into a run when doing civilian rescue work; a run indicated alarm, and when civilians saw uniformed men run they panicked. They walked across the intersection, dodging the cars. The policeman saw the uniformed men and went on clicking his switch.

"Hold off! Get back! Stop!" the officer commanded the river of people flowing along the sidewalk directly into the flailing pile of bodies. He ducked into a doorway, called up command on the walkie-talkie, and asked for help.

"Headquarters will send reinforcements from Depot A. We'll hold off this mob in the meantime!" he shouted to the private, switching off the set.

"Yes, sir!"

"Get back," he roared at the shoving, yelling crowd. It was useless. People swirled around the corner and piled into those struggling and yelling on the sidewalk. The people beneath were in the death throes of asphyxiation. The young lieutenant drew his revolver. Those in front pushed on, not seeing. The next wave came face to face with the lieutenant, his features angrily tight. It was something new for him to be disobeyed.

"One step and I'll fire!" he cried.

A youth, swept along in the crush, saw the revolver and flung his fist at it. The gun fired. The youth crumpled, the side of his face blown away. The oncoming crowd hesitated, then rammed forward as those behind shoved harder. The

EPICENTER

air filled with shrieks and moans, plate-glass windows cracked and shattered into sharp-edged pieces that crashed into the crowd, but the officer held his ground.

The policeman looked anxiously across the intersection. He'd heard the shot, but the cars cut off his line of vision. He saw the heads of the two soldiers and figured they had everything under control, the shot was a warning. He heard the horn of a large military truck blasting along Queen Street and hurriedly switched the lights to clear a way for it, but it took fifteen minutes for the truck to reach the intersection. By the time troop reinforcements arrived all they could do was to cordon off the area, cart off the dead, and load as many of the injured as they could in the back of their truck.

"There are two main areas of concern right now," Ferrisston continued. "One is to ensure that the reception centers are set up and ready. The other, I understand from our Ottawa representatives, is to decide on what to do at Fairfield. Atomic Energy Control Board has been fully informed of the accident, and representatives are now on their way from Ottawa by air to this center. First, can we have a report from federal health and welfare?"

A thin man rose and shuffled some papers.

"It's okay to sit," Ferrisston said stiffly.

"I was in touch by telephone with the provincial officials before I left Ottawa," the man said in a firm voice. "The whole of the federal program is now operating. Clearing stations for casualties are being set up at Brampton, Schomberg, Bolton, and Uxbridge. The centers at Barrie and Orillia are being kept as reserves. Feeding stations will be established near each casualty center. Provincial EMO say that most casualties are expected to come from the area immediately west of Fairfield." He paused, tapping a pencil lightly on the table.

"Is EMO doing remedial evacuation right now, Mr. Ferrisston?" A heavy, dark-skinned man was speaking from the opposite side of the table. He looked familiar to Johnson—it was that fellow from the regional transportation office who had contacted him once about trucking some big pressure vessels down to Fairfield. They had been too wide for the maximum allowable legal load and he had had to get special permission and then had had to move them at night, when traffic was light. A good man. Sliced through red tape.

"Remedial evacuation is going on at present," Ferrisston said decisively, his voice sharply irritated. He turned to Johnson.

"You gentlemen who were at the power station have been brought here for the obvious reason that you can give us valuable advice on the technical aspects of the accident." His voice softened slightly as he peered over his oversize eyeglasses.

"As soon as some lines are free on the main switchboard you can phone home. I would think that under the circumstances your families have already evacuated. I understand your feelings—many of us here are in the same boat. When your Ottawa colleagues arrive we'll get on with discussing the best way to stop the radiation from the station. Unless you'd like to start now?"

"Who's coming?" Johnson demanded curtly.

"The Atomic Energy Control Board representatives for a start," Ferrisston replied officiously. He picked up the telephone at his elbow. "Ferrisston here. What's the latest on arrival of the Atomic Control People?" He listened. "Thanks," he said, and replaced the instrument.

"They left Toronto International in a CH-53 five minutes

ago. Be here in six minutes. I suggest we stretch our legs a bit before they arrive. We can go into the hall."

Johnson caught Townsend's eye and nodded toward the door as they moved outside with the others. The hallway was crowded with EMO officials and provincial police officers who hurried at drill pace from one doorway to another.

"That'll be Deighton for sure," Johnson told Townsend. "Buck up, he'll cut through this baloney." He nodded toward the conference room. "He's got authority to override EMO, I would guess."

"I hope so, sir. They're treating it like a war game, some sort of exercise. They don't realize—"

A motorcycle policeman with snow on his leggings clattered down the steps clutching an envelope in his gloved hand. He went up to Ferrisston, who was just coming out, saluted, and gave it to him. Ferrisston fished his glasses from under his topcoat and swiftly put them on, tore open the envelope, and read the note inside.

"There's no reply," he told the policeman, who left immediately. Ferrisston slowly removed his glasses and put them in an inside pocket. His eyes were glazed. Johnson's attention was suddenly diverted by the fluph-fluph-fluph of a helicopter rotor approaching overhead. He heard the bass tone of the engine, then it died. They were guided into a larger room where there was a long table with chairs around it, a huge map of Metropolitan Toronto and outskirts on the wall, and a rank of telephones and colored lights on a console at the head of the table. The only sound in the room was a slight hum from the air-conditioning system. Ferrisston pressed past and stood in front of the map.

"Be seated, gentlemen," he said, his voice husky. "I've just received confirmation from sector control of an earlier radio message from the director general of Ottawa EMO that the

EPICENTER

Prime Minister has declared Toronto a disaster area. The full facilities of the EMO at all three levels of government have been put at the disposal of the area command." He looked around the long oblong of faces at the table and added: "The Atomic Energy Control people have arrived with other officials. They'll be here in a moment."

Joe Griffiths was a member of the EMO Rescue Team based in Willowdale in north Toronto. He sat in a covered truck with nine other men, bumping toward Fairfield to carry out remedial evacuation of the citizens. His vehicle was one of many racing to the same district from other depots.

Remedial evacuation. The term had been raising eyebrows and tempers in EMO headquarters and lecture sessions for years. Ottawa had removed Toronto and other cities from its list of primary enemy nuclear targets in case of war. The argument was that if an enemy wanted to knock out the United States with nuclear missiles, why waste ammunition on Canada? Aim for the bigger industrial targets—New York, Chicago, Pittsburgh, Detroit, Los Angeles, and, of course, Washington. Nuclear bombs dropped on Toronto, Winnipeg, Montreal, or Vancouver would knock out Canada, but Canada would more easily become useless as an ally of the west without dropping a single bomb on her territory —by spreading nuclear devastation throughout the United States. Canada was economically and strategically tied to the United States; destroy the American ability to fight, and the Canadian collapse would automatically follow. Thus it had been decided to soft-pedal the evacuation angle. Instead, the local EMO's were to concentrate on remedial evacuation.

Riding in the truck now, Griffiths' mind went back to his EMO class a few years back, at the time the decision had been made. "If a nuclear bomb lands smack in the center of a city like Montreal or Toronto there's no point in total evacuation," the lecturer had explained to the class. "People in the center will be killed, and those immediately outside will die from radiation sickness. But the people in the out-lying fringe areas—they would likely be okay if you can get them out in time. That's what we mean by remedial evacuation."

Griffiths looked across at John Anders, the rescue team captain sent with him from Toronto to the Arnprior College, and made a helpless gesture with his shoulders. Anders smiled and raised his eyebrows.

Griffiths had wondered how the young lecturer, fresh from his passing-out examinations, would react under action. The room was overheated, and his attention began to wane.

"The victims in the center would be killed instantaneously and those just outside would be irradiated. Then there's the danger from the firestorm . . ."

This grim observation had made Griffiths remember a night when fire bombs had fallen on London when he was a young man during World War II working with the civil defense rescue team. The raid had been particularly heavy—first a rain of incendiaries, then high-explosive bombs to stir things up. He'd been sent to a street near Oxford Circus, where a high-explosive bomb had glanced off a row of Edwardian houses and crashed through roadworks in the street. It had broken open a sewer and water mains, flooding a section of an Underground station that had been sealed off at both ends to provide a safe place for people to sleep. A demolition cap-tain had approached Griffiths.

"Ever been in a diver's suit, young 'un?" he'd shouted above the shattering roar of the anti-aircraft guns and the crunch of bombs exploding some distance away.

"Nope!"

EPICENTER

"Well, 'ere's your chance!" the captain had yelled.

Before Griffiths had known what was happening he was in an old-fashioned diver's suit and a metal helmet was being screwed over his head. A rubber hose pumped in air and he was hoisted through an opening in what had been until recently the flower-bordered front garden of a demolished house. They thrust a flashlight into his hand. His feet hit water, and he found himself in a turbid green world where more than two hundred drowned bodies were swirling around. His job was to fish them out.

"They all floated up to the top," he explained years later. "There were women with their arms around babies, and small kids with their hands clutching each other. I remember one man had a fearful grin on his face, like a laughing ghost. I think it would have been quick. The water poured in all of a sudden."

Back in the classroom, the instructor's voice had droned on in textbook boredom. "Remedial evacuation would have as its objectives the evacuation of people in the irradiated border perimeter. There may be cases where people refuse to leave their homes. In such cases force may have to be applied . . ."

The scene inside Griffiths' mind had changed with those words, and he thought of a house in North Kensington that had been hit, a freak strike. The lower part of the house had been partially blown away by the blast, leaving the top story swaying on top of crumbling bricks and mortar. By the time Griffiths had arrived the members of the civil defense rescue team were being thrown out of the remains of the house by the eighty-five-year-old woman who owned it.

"I was carried into this 'ouse as a bride sixty-six years ago," she had cried indignantly. " 'Itler couldn't get me out and I'm sure you ain't!"

The men had backed away, and Griffiths had peered inside

107

the wrecked downstairs. Miraculously, most of the furniture was not seriously damaged.

"The mayor's down the street talking to the fire fighters, madam. Would you like to talk to him about it?" he had asked the old lady.

"You bet I would!" she had croaked sharply. "It's disgusting trying to turn a poor old woman out of 'er own 'ouse, and after all these years!"

She had wrapped a coat around her shoulders and stepped delicately over the debris. When she had gone two hundred yards the team had whisked the furniture out of the remains of the house, laid dynamite charges, and blown the swaying structure into fragments. The old woman had whirled around. "My 'ouse! My 'ouse!" she had cried, tears pouring down her face. "You've gone and blown up my 'ouse!" She had sobbed on the shoulder of a civil defense man, stamping her foot and swaying back and forth with grief.

Griffiths was brought up short in his reveries when the truck suddenly stopped. "Looks like a traffic jam this way," the driver called out. "I'll try down here." He swung the wheel and drove along a side street to get past the lines of stopped vehicles ahead. The truck was approaching the border of Fairfield, and cars were racing northward to Highway 401. At this point 401 was close to Lake Ontario because of the indentations of a wide bay. The power station was on the edge of the bay, where cooling water could be pumped from the lake. During the past few years housing developments had crept near the 3,000-foot demarcation line around the reactor buildings, the distance specified by the authorities as being the safe limit for building residences.

Griffiths caught sight of three other EMO trucks, two of them carrying rescue appliances, following some distance away.

"There're the others," he shouted to Anders, who sat in front. He raised his thumb in acknowledgment.

Griffiths looked at the sky. It was still dark overhead, and the streetlights were on. There was no sign of smoke. He'd half expected the lights to be out with the power station not operating.

Many of the houses were dark, their occupants gone. But as the truck approached the station more of the smaller homes were lit up and cars were parked in the driveways. The truck stopped, waiting for the others to catch up.

A group of people were standing around the front door of a bungalow watching, with an air of contempt, Griffiths and Anders approach.

"Haven't you heard about the evacuation order? Everybody's got to leave. There's been an accident at the power station," Anders said.

"Yep! We heard. But we've decided to stay!" a middle-aged man replied, jutting his jaw defiantly.

"I'm sorry, sir. There are no exceptions. There's a radioactive cloud coming this way and it's deadly poisonous. We've got orders to make sure everybody's out."

"Is that so? Like I said, we've decided to stay, haven't we?"

The others nodded. "I can't see no radioactive cloud coming this way," a skinny woman smirked. Griffiths smelled beer on her breath. He tried to look inside the house, but the glass on the storm door was steamed over.

"Joe, go back to the truck and radio to Armed Forces headquarters. Tell 'em we need help," Anders ordered. He turned to the group. "Our orders are to evacuate everybody in the area. Other rescue teams are making sure that all Toronto's evacuated. You may not be able to see the radioactivity," he pointed skyward, "but it's coming this way fast. And it'll kill you if you stay!"

"I'm going to catch up on some sleep. Gotta be at work by eight. You folks goin' home?" the woman asked, looking at her neighbors and yawning.

"Yep. Early to bed an' early to rise—" another cackled drunkenly.

They opened the door and went inside, and their friends disappeared into the bungalow next door.

The other trucks slid up to Anders' and stopped. Anders ordered one truck to remain outside the bungalow with instructions to the man in charge to wait until the soldiers came. "If they won't go in their own cars, put 'em in the truck and take 'em to the nearest bus center," he said grimly before moving off with his own truck and the second vehicle.

"Suits on!" Anders yelled through the cab window. The truck stopped. The driver put on a plastic protective suit and pulled the hood over his head. Anders took a geiger counter from its case on top of the dashboard and Griffiths removed the lid of a box in the back of the truck and handed everyone a portable counter. Anders looked through the rear window to check that the men had their suits on.

As they approached the district near the power station they found more groups of people clustered around front porches or talking in groups in the middle of the road. Anders picked up the microphone of the headquarters radio set.

"We need a blanket warning system over Fairfield district. People won't evacuate. Send the aerial warning system," he told the operator at the other end urgently.

"Are you right in the area?" a gruff voice crackled from the speaker.

"Yes. We've put protective suits on."

"Sorry. We can't fly the aircraft in your area. The radioactivity's too hot for it. You'd better use the bullhorn."

Anders swore and switched off. He'd forgotten about the

low-altitude aerial pollution—an aircraft flying low in the area would be contaminated. He'd wanted the blanket warning system—a speaker towed below a low-flying light plane—to reach everybody in the neighborhood. Now he faced the prospect of prying out the stick-ins separately, resorting to force or having to call in troops if his team failed. He grasped the electric bullhorn firmly and aimed it out of the window.

"This is Emergency Measures calling. There is a general evacuation order. Everybody must leave their homes immediately. Fairfield Nuclear Power Station is discharging deadly radioactivity into the air. The station has been abandoned. Everyone must leave. It's for your own safety. If you remain you could die or be seriously sick through radioactivity." He spoke slowly, pronouncing each word deliberately.

Griffiths watched a knot of people in front of a house who turned and looked interestedly at the truck as it slowly passed. How different from the sudden explosive blasts and roaring fires of the air raids. This was an invisible attacker. There were no crashing and exploding bombs to make people take split-second action, no fire to drive them, terror-stricken, into the street. Just wailing sirens and announcements, almost like watchmen calling alarums in the night. The danger was unseen, unheard, unfelt—at least in the beginning. An utter intangible. Funny, too, that the nearer the source of danger the more indifferent people were. The old woman's face from North Kensington again burst into his mind. He drew back from the pout of her lip and the vivid flashing eyes, and heard her shrill cry as he blew up her home.

Anders ordered the truck to stop and put the counter outside the window. The needle showed above normal and the instrument clicked ominously. He grabbed the bullhorn.

"The radioactivity's increasing in this district. Everybody must leave. EMO orders everyone to leave now. Reception areas for everybody are being set up north of the city. If you don't have a car, go to the nearest bus terminal. Buses leave from Greenwood Racetrack. Repeat, it is dangerous to stay in your homes. This is an EMO order, everybody—"

A car raced down a side street and braked in a skidding curve toward the truck. Anders flung the instrument on the seat beside him, instinctively hugging the driver. The car struck the truck's right fender and ricocheted off. Then it shot across the road, raced over a front garden, and rammed into a brick house. Anders tried to open the truck door but it was stuck.

"Out the other way, Bill!" he shouted to the driver. Griffiths reached the car first and peered inside. The driver's head hung over the dashboard, blood dripping from a cracked skull. The face of the young woman beside him was smashed against the shattered windshield. A mattress, two flight bags, and some parcels lay in a heap in the back. One of the flight bags had ripped open, spilling the woman's clothing on the car floor.

Griffiths wrenched the partly open front door. He swept back the woman's hair, pulled up her eyelid. "She's dead," he said. "Killed on impact."

"He's still living!" Anders exclaimed, lifting the man's head. His hands were slimy with blood. "Get the stretchers." Someone went back to the truck.

A few people approached, their faces stimulated by morbid curiosity. "Clear the way," Anders ordered, seizing the microphone. As the injured man was put on the stretcher and the body removed, Armed Forces trucks roared around the corner and stopped. A platoon of soldiers tumbled out and a lieutenant hurried up.

"What's this?" he asked quietly.

"The car hit our truck, bounced off," Anders replied. "She's dead, he's got to get to a hospital right away. The people around here won't evacuate. We need your help."

The lieutentant was about twenty-eight, well built, and efficient-looking. He glanced around, sizing things up. Some cars down the street started to move off. The lights were on in the houses opposite. He looked across the road, then back to the stretchers being loaded into the truck.

"Get one of your men to drive the injured man to the hospital at Uxbridge," he told Anders. "It's about forty miles. We'll take care of these people. Leave as many of your men here as possible—I may need them. Where're your other trucks? Didn't you have a group of three?" He spoke with self-assurance, aware of what had been planned.

"We were separated." Anders made a hopeless gesture. "We've told everybody here by bullhorn they must go. Some have, but you can see for yourself—"

"We'll fix it," the lieutenant said grimly.

Griffiths was in the small group that stayed when Anders dispatched the truck to Uxbridge. "You come with me," the lieutenant said to Griffiths. "You take the other side of the street," he said to Anders. They joined the soldiers who were wearing plastic suits and hoods, at the military truck. A sergeant monitored the radiation level with a portable counter.

"Radiation getting high here, sir," he announced as the lieutenant approached.

"Let's get going," the officer snapped. "Sergeant, take eight men and go along the street from this point," he indicated with his arm. "Knock on every door where there's a light. If anybody answers tell them they've got to leave immediately. Allow them three minutes to pack necessities. If they're not out by then use force. No unnecessary force," he added.

"Yes, sir," the sergeant said smartly.

"You men," the lieutenant continued, looking at Griffiths and the others, "come with me and the rest of my men. We'll take the next street. We'll have to winkle them out street by street if necessary."

Lights were on in the first house but the occupants had fled. Next door, in a story-and-a-half frame house, an elderly man dressed in a sweat shirt and soiled baggy trousers answered the heavy knocking.

"Sorry, sir, you must leave. Haven't you heard?" the lieutenant said sharply.

The man raised a hand to cup his ear. "Wha's 'at?"

"You'll have to leave. There's been an accident at the power station."

The man looked past the lieutenant. His eyes opened wide at the sight of the armed soldiers in the narrow driveway.

"What's all them fellas doin'? 'As there bin an invasion or somethin'?"

The lieutenant gulped a deep breath. "Anybody else live here?" he asked abruptly.

"Eh?"

The lieutenant took a step toward the old man.

"Who else lives here?" he yelled in his ear.

"Only the missus an' me."

"Where is she?"

"Eh?"

"Where's your missus?" the lieutenant barked loudly.

"Oh—she's upstairs."

"Is she awake? She'll have to go with you." The lieutenant turned to the men behind him. "Sergeant, tell the corporal to take four men to the next house. We'll handle this one ourselves." He turned to the old man.

"Tell your wife she'll have to leave with you." He pointed at his watch. "Be ready in three minutes. Do you have a car?"

EPICENTER

The lieutenant swung around and his question was answered. There was no car in the driveway, and no garage.

"Now see here, young fella. You 'aven't got no right to turn me and the missus out of me own 'ouse. You got no right." The old man's voice quavered indignantly. Griffiths, in the driveway, suddenly felt sick, and looked away.

The lieutenant stepped across the threshold, waving for his men to follow. The old man retreated into the narrow hall. "You can't come barging in 'ere without a search warrant. I know my rights," he yelled in a cracked, hoarse voice. "I'll write to my MP."

"This is an emergency," the lieutenant said as evenly as he could. "Didn't you hear the sirens and the announcements on the radio?"

"Eh? Wha's 'at you say? Radio. We 'aven't got no radio. We can't 'ear none too well. The missus, she's stone deaf."

"Now, tell your wife she has to leave with you. We'll arrange to take you to a reception center. You can come back to your home as soon as the emergency's over. Everybody's got to get out of Toronto." The lieutenant spoke the words deliberately into the old man's ear, cupping his hands together to make a crude trumpet.

The old man's eyes narrowed. He drew himself up straight and looked into the lieutenant's young face.

"Get out of Trona? We ain't goin' nowhere!" he shouted defiantly.

"You and you," the lieutenant said firmly, pointing to two of his men. "Get the old lady down here. We'll look after the old man."

The two men ran up the stairs, their boots echoing noisily on the threadbare carpet. The old man turned to stop them, but the sergeant pulled his arm.

"Hey! Let go! Blast your eyes!" the old man yelled. "Come down 'ere. My missus is sleeping up there."

When the two soldiers appeared on the landing they held an old women between them, her frail form wrapped in a worn pink dressing gown, gray hair streaming over her face. She blabbered incoherently.

"Better carry her down," the sergeant ordered. He turned to the lieutenant. "What about food and things, sir?"

"No time. Get them in the truck and let's get on," he replied, glancing at the geiger counter.

"Hey! Put my missus down!" the old man cried. He struggled free and pummeled the face of one of the soldiers carrying his wife. The soldier warded off the blows with the butt of his automatic rifle. Downstairs another soldier opened the hall closet, looking for the woman's coat.

"Get out of there! You ain't got no right. I'll see my lawyer!" the old man shouted feebly, running with tottering steps to the soldier rummaging through the closet.

"Look, dad—I only want to make sure your old lady gets something warm on before we evacuate her," the soldier said insolently.

"Let's get going," the lieutenant said. "No unnecessary force." Turning to the old man, he said, "It's an order. We're only carrying out orders. Everybody has to evacuate—the whole city."

The soldiers carried the dazed old woman down the driveway to the waiting truck. The sergeant slammed the front door, and the old man hobbled down the snow-covered path, trying to catch up with them, his bony fingers struggling to button the frayed edges of his topcoat.

Ferrisston's voice had a whiplike quality that cut through the tense atmosphere in the conference room.

EPICENTER

"The police chief of the Metropolitan area reports that evacuation is still proceeding but there have been some delays caused by traffic jams," he said.

"What about the radioactivity from Fairfield" demanded a bony-faced man with a huge graying mustache that exaggerated his gaunt look. He was Richard L. Deighton.

"Here's a report from the armed forces radiation squad— it's just come in," Ferrisston replied, picking up a sheet of yellow paper an aide had put in front of him.

"The radioactivity level across Highway 2 near the Scarborough Golf Club was reported at a dangerously high level at—uh, let me see—about twenty minutes ago. A mile further west, near the railway tracks where they cross Eglinton Avenue, the level was also at a danger level, enough to cause long-term radiation burns. Farther west again, at the junction of—"

"Excuse my butting in," Deighton interrupted impatiently. Ferrisston's roundabout way of talking irritated him, and he had come to the same conclusion Johnson had: Ferrisston's authoritative manner covered up what he suspected to be a profound ignorance of the technicalities of the nuclear hazard. "Does that report give any idea of the width of the plume that's coming from Fairfield? Is it spreading sideways?"

"As far as we can ascertain, the plume, as you refer to it, is fairly narrow," Ferrisston replied. "A monitoring report from Highway 401 directly north of the golf club shows radiation above normal but not at the danger level." He waved a pencil in the air negatively.

"That doesn't mean anything," Deighton snapped. "The plume could be leveling off at a higher altitude and widening over the lake. The bay sweeps up at that point." He pointed to the map behind Ferrisston.

Ferrisston swung around so that everybody could see the

117

map. He put the pencil hesitantly on a point north of the golf club.

"Have you got anybody monitoring down here?" Deighton demanded, striding to the map and indicating with a broad sweep of his hand the lakeside and the inshore waters of Lake Ontario.

"Nothing here. These are the Scarborough Bluffs here, a residential area that's been evacuated. The only way we could monitor over the lake would be by shipborne equipment. We haven't any," Ferrisston replied, his long legs apart in an elemental defensive posture.

"What's your latest meteorological report?" Deighton asked in a commanding tone. At the Control Board he had a reputation for hanging on by the teeth to a line of questioning until he was satisfied. Johnson watched the power struggle between the two men with detached interest, despite the concern with death, lingering overdoses of radiation, and the potential breakdown of organized local government.

Ferrisston picked up one of the telephones. When he spoke his voice was quieter. A moment later the door opened and an aide brought in the latest weather report. Ferrisston read it aloud: "Freshening easterly wind, seven to ten miles an hour. Wind veering slightly during the day with possibility of snow precipitation toward the afternoon."

He looked around the room. There were twenty or more men before him, representing specialized knowledge in several fields. He was fighting to regain the initiative, but when he spoke his voice had a dull edge. He realized that he now depended on expert knowledge he didn't have.

"The first thing we have to consider now that evacuation is proceeding is how to stop the leak from Fairfield. Can we have an expression of opinion from the Control Board officials?

Our plan to allow people back into the city depends, of course, on when the radioactive leak is brought to an end."

"I'm worried about the changing wind forecast," Deighton said imperiously. "When the snow falls through the radio-activity we're going to get a carpet of long-term irradiation on the ground, including rooftops, sidewalks, and streets. When it thaws it'll go down the storm sewers and be washed out into the lake. For a short time radioactivity may increase in local inshore waters, then be diffused. I mention this to acquaint EMO people here with the prospect. The other thing I want to mention at this stage, before we discuss ending the cause of the radioactivity, is the effect of temperature and wind changes on the escaping poisons." He paused and looked at Johnson. "Johnson here is our expert on these matters. Will you explain, please?"

Johnson rose. The question had caught him off guard. The lecture Deighton had given at the control operators' course years ago flashed through his mind. The man had a phenomenal memory! He'd recalled the thesis Johnson had given on wind-carried radiation. Deighton had taken a rigid position, which Johnson had slowly eroded by a brilliant discussion. In the end Deighton had conceded that he had been wrong.

"There are five ways the wind can affect what's flowing out of Fairfield right at this moment," Johnson said clearly. "They're called fanning, looping, coning, lofting, and fumigation. Let's eliminate them one by one, then we can judge the danger." He stopped to swallow. Ferrisston seized the chance to butt in.

"Are you saying the leak's going to take a long time to fix?" he asked bluntly, leaning forward.

Johnson didn't reply immediately. Deighton caught his eye and some unspoken understanding passed between them.

EPICENTER

"We think the explanation is important because it can affect EMO's operations today. If the leak persists—say for a few days—the wind conditions will have a strong bearing on your rescue teams. No—I'm not saying the leak's going to take a long time to fix, but I can't say how long it'll take to fix." He carefully chose Ferrisston's own phrases to answer him. He didn't want him to think he was not getting a direct answer. Ferrisston sat back in his chair.

"I'd say the leak's fanning right now," Johnson continued. "At dawn the air is usually stable. The radioactivity is probably streaming away in a thin layer and spreading sideways like a fan." Johnson got down to basics, paring a difficult subject to the bone.

"If the temperature falls off rapidly with height, we'd get a condition called looping. The stream from the chimney outlets at the station will loop low to the ground, then swing high, like a deep wave. It may rise clear over some houses and bear down on others."

He looked around at the tired faces. Ferrisston now sat with his head on his hand. Despite the strain, everybody in the room was paying close attention.

"Then there is coning. The smoke from the chimney makes a cone shape as it's swept downwind—spreading out sideways, upward, and downward."

He paused to make sure everybody understood. "After that we have lofting. This could trap the contaminated air at a certain level as it flows in a thin layer from the chimneys, like cigarette smoke in a calm room."

He picked up a pencil from the table and moved to the map, his face grim. When he spoke, his voice was confidential as the atmosphere tensed.

"The worst condition we may have to deal with is fumigation, from an upper-air inversion, with a layer of radioactive air trapped between layers of warm and cool air. As the air comes from the chimneys it rolls over the ground like a heavy poison gas." He swept the pencil in a huge arc over the map from the Fairfield district toward downtown Toronto.

There was a hush in the room. Johnson was conscious of a noisy air-conditioning fan in a far-off duct. Then Ferrisston spoke.

"Is that what killed five thousand people in London some years ago when they couldn't get rid of the trapped smog?" he asked.

"Yes. But from your met report I believe we can forget an inversion of that size," Johnson continued. "The air is fairly stable this time of year. But we can expect coning. It means that the air close to the ground about"—he blew out his lips, studying the map intently—"about half a mile away, assuming a ten-mile-an-hour wind, would get a fairly concentrated dose of contamination."

He returned quickly to his seat. Deighton glanced at him before rising.

"It's a very serious condition," Deighton snapped. "I want to hear from our radiation-protection services." He had all but become chairman of the meeting now that the discussion was on his own subject. A small, ferretlike man got to his feet amid the clatter of shifting chairs.

"Our main concern is to get dosimeters and whole-body counters on the people evacuated from the irradiated areas around Fairfield as soon as possible. It's as simple as that," he said in a raspy voice.

Whole-body counters! Johnson suddenly caught a whiff of the odor of death and abruptly his mind went back to the time he'd visited the Hiroshima Peace Memorial Museum. He'd been in Tokyo as a member of a technical mission trying to sell nuclear reactors to the Japanese. On the weekend he had left the group and flown to Hiroshima because he had a strong compulsion to visit the rebuilt city. What he saw distressed him. He had stood in front of the glass showcases with a hard lump in his throat, and he wasn't the only one.

"I fought them in the Solomons, but it was nothing like this," a tall fresh-faced man near him had muttered, his features distorted. Johnson recognized the Australian drawl.

In the glass cases before him was a realistic lifesize dummy of a woman, her blue dress burned and torn, revealing flesh fried into horrible purplish keloids. A ticket gave her name and age, forty-one, and simply stated that she'd been waiting for a train at Hiroshima Station at eight fifteen one August morning a long time ago, waiting for a train that never came.

A young girl's once-black hair, now dull brown, was pressed between two layers of glass in another showcase. "The hair fell from a survivor's scalp," he had read on the ticket.

The radiation expert was still talking, bringing Johnson back to the present crisis. "It's important that all the people evacuated from around Fairfield and westward—possibly as far west as the center of the city—be tested by whole-body counters," the expert was saying. "The big problem is that they're being dispersed all over the place. Is there any way of locating these people quickly?" He sat down, his slight figure looking forlorn at the end of the table.

"No way at all," replied Ferrisston, in a booming voice, trying to regain his leadership of the group. "They could end up in half a dozen different reception areas. But we'll be able to pinpoint some of them easily enough. I have here a report from the remedial-evacuation task force. It says many people around the power station won't budge. We're having to use force to get them out and have called in the Armed Forces for help."

"Isn't it possible to transport them to one or two reception areas instead of spreading them around? We'd be able to test them for radiation quicker and save lives," the radiation specialist said urgently.

Johnson swallowed and the saliva stuck in his throat. He thought about Rita. She would have returned from Barbados by now, and he wondered what she had done when the sirens went off. She might have ignored the panic and stayed behind. Something like that would suit her stubborn independence. If she had remained she'd be in danger. Some of the men around this table might be bumbling from one crisis to another, but he reckoned that Deighton at least knew what he was talking about. With a freshening wind the whole of the Metropolitan Toronto area would very soon be enveloped in a highly dangerous radioactive atmosphere. He looked up at the overhead lights and began to bite his fingernails.

Ferrisston snapped up the telephone and barked an order.

"Instruct all personnel on remedial evacuation to take the evacuees to either the Schomberg or Uxbridge reception centers, preferably Uxbridge," he said tersely. His ruddy complexion was showing signs of strain, and shadows now underlined his eyes. He replaced the receiver and looked up as an aide entered, laid a sheaf of report forms on the table, and left. Ferrisston picked them up as he put on his glasses. Deighton shifted restlessly and opened his mouth to speak, but Ferrisston got there first.

"These are reports on the progress of the evacuation. Remedial evacuation is still running into opposition in some localities, particularly around Fairfield. Lord! Can't they see they've got to get out?" Johnson was struck with the ineptness of the remark. The contaminated air was invisible; the potential victims could see nothing alarming. "There are still traffic tieups in many parts of the metropolitan area with some local breakdown in law and order. Here—here's a report of one incident. In a three-car collision on Highway 401 north of the city a man drew a gun on the driver who smashed into the car in which he was a passenger. He went berserk and shot the man. The gunman was trying to run from the crashed car at the time, but he had an injured leg. He escaped. No details are available. Here's another report about a woman driver murdered . . ."

"Can we press on with the state of Fairfield now, Mr. Chairman?" Deighton asked sharply.

"I was coming to that—" Ferrisston began.

"I think Mr. Johnson should give us a report on what happened at the station," Deighton interrupted. Ferrisston waved his hand wearily.

Johnson felt a spasm in his viscera, and his face looked pained. He gave an account of the happenings at the station from the time he had heard MacGregor's voice on the telephone reporting that the fuel bundles had stuck somewhere in the chute to the moment Townsend gave the signal to abandon the station.

When he finished, the atmosphere in the room was clammy. Johnson could hear only the whirl of the distant air-conditioning fan—it was being driven too fast, he noted to himself; they should sound-baffle the outlets. Deighton thanked him.

"You were all lucky to get away in time. There must have been radioactive iodine in the ventilating system as well as gamma-ray-contaminated dust particles," he said thoughtfully. "You've all been tested, of course?"

"Yes. As soon as we arrived, we used the airport's monitoring equipment," Johnson replied, referring to the monitoring instruments maintained at most international airports handling transoceanic and transcontinental flights. Aircraft flying at heights over 30,000 feet are sometimes exposed to radioactive fallout that swirls through the earth's upper atmosphere from the hydrogen bombs exploded by the Chinese. When the aircraft land they are quietly gone over with dosimeters and hosed down with clean water to wash off contamination.

The telephone in front of Ferrisston rang shrilly. He picked it up and listened intently. There was a long silence. "Yes—I can summarize the facts very swiftly for him. Yes, federal, provincial, and municipal government representatives are all here, also the staff from Fairfield. I'll switch on the PA system so we can all hear." He spoke crisply, flicked a switch on the console, and his voice broke out into the room from hidden speakers. He covered the mouthpiece with his hand. "It's General Waring, National Director of EMO, Ottawa. The Minister of National Defense is also on the line," he said quickly, then realizing that he need not cover the telephone with the PA system on, returned it to his ear.

"Ferrisston. This is General Waring. Understand you've got the Fairfield control staff with you. And that evacuation is still proceeding but you've got problems." He sounded gruff through the speakers.

Ferrisston hesitated a moment. "That's correct, sir, but when there's more light I believe we'll be able to clear up the tough spots. We were just about to discuss methods of stopping the leak at the power station."

"Good. We have a closed-circuit wire system set up here with lines into the Atomic Energy labs at Chalk River. The scientific staff there have been alerted and are standing by. The Prime Minister was advised of the situation as soon as your order for the siren alert was given . . ."

"My siren alert? You must mean the Attorney General's, sir," Ferrisston broke in, sitting up like an uncoiled spring.

"Yes—but you gave the advice to the Attorney General directly, I take it, in accordance with standing instructions," Waring said. A shadow of doubt had seeped into his voice.

"Right, but it was the Attorney General who contacted the Brigadier General for the Ontario Region Command. Presumably he got clearance for the first siren from Ottawa," Ferrisston shot back, his voice edged with a corrosive bite.

"We won't argue at this stage of the game about who's responsible for what. If there's been some foul-up we'll deal with it at the public enquiry," the general said in a more sonorous tone.

"Public enquiry, sir?"

"Yes—there'll be one about the accident at Fairfield. Not until the leak's fixed, of course."

When the procedure for dealing with warlike acts against the state had been drafted for the War Book, the rights of the provinces had been studiously observed. Neither the federal government nor the provincial governments had any legal right to declare martial law. The civil authority was supreme: only Parliament could declare martial law. However, for protection against insurrection or armed rebellion, the Attorney General of a province could seek help from the military commander of an area. This officer could then commit troops without having first to ask federal government permission.

But for the ordinary maintenance of law and order, legally referred to as giving aid to the civil power, the military commander first had to obtain clearance from the federal government before he could order the troops out.

The thinking within EMO had undergone various changes. After the decision had been made to scrap the total evacuation of cities and rely on remedial evacuation, it was easy for regional EMO commissioners to realign their thinking, but this procedure had never been called upon to deal with a peacetime disaster such as Fairfield. The result had been muddled thinking: the military commander had exceeded his authority when he had sounded the sirens at the request of the Attorney General.

After a pause General Waring's voice boomed through the room again. "We've got to get that leak stopped! It's not EMO's direct responsibility, but the government is giving it the first priority while EMO looks after the evacuee problem. Now that we've all hooked up, give us a rundown on what went on at Fairfield. Then you nuclear people had better take the floor and suggest how you're going to clean up the mess."

Ferrisston quickly summed up the night's events, repeated Johnson's main points from notes he'd taken, and waited expectantly for the report from the nuclear experts at Atomic Energy laboratories.

"We could build a lead-sheathed structure around the dropped fuel bundles and the smashed shielding and cut off the radioactivity right at the source." A well-modulated English voice sounded through the speaker system. It was calm, almost casual, as though discussing a cricket game at teabreak.

"The point's well taken about cutting it off at the source," Deighton replied, recognizing the voice as belonging to his opposite number at the labs. "Trouble is, how do you start to build such a structure? It's very hot at the source—probably too hot for standard protective clothing." He spoke loudly to make sure the remote microphones picked up his voice.

Johnson interrupted: "We could push it to a suitable burial place with bulldozers fitted with lead-lined buckets and lead protective shielding for the operators. I don't agree with leaving the radiation source inside the station perimeter." He was anxious to make his position known early on.

"Actually, there'd be no danger to the station if they were sealed up on the premises," the English voice replied.

"If I may make a suggestion," Townsend said. Ferrisston

nodded. "We could simulate the waste-fuel-tank system, where bundles are kept underwater, by building a dike at some safe distance around the bundles and then flooding the area inside the dike. We might even put a lead-lined roof over it by building some sort of bridge structure."

There was a momentary pause. The first line of suggestions, clever in their way, had exhausted the obvious solutions that sprang instantly to the minds of men trained in engineering. One by one they had been discarded by the need to take extraordinary precautions against the concentrated radioactivity pouring from the Fairfield site.

"The ventilating system at the station must be thoroughly contaminated by now," somebody broke the silence on the wires.

"You've got to get those bundles right out of there!" General Waring's voice boomed out, vibrating the speakers with a tinny resonance. "That's basic! I don't know how you're going to do it—that's your problem. If the radioactivity coming from the station isn't stopped soon I'll have to order evacuation of an even bigger area than Metropolitan Toronto!"

EIGHT

The snores of the slumbering people in the school hall woke Rita before two o'clock. The same sounds and the stifling air in the overheated room had disturbed her sleep for the past three nights. She lay in the hard bunk, hands under her head, thinking things over. The radio had earlier announced the latest news about the contamination over Toronto. She didn't think it would last more than another day or two; a wind would get up and blow the radioactive material away. She'd read the exaggerated accounts of the first reports that came from Hiroshima, stating categorically that people would never be able to live anywhere near the devastated city for fifty years or more, and how, in fact, life had returned to some semblance of normality just a few months after the catastrophe. She didn't believe the tales of horror that had shaken some people in the schoolhouse yesterday, despite the grim lettering on the trucks in the yard outside. An ambulance attendant had brought back a story about hundreds of people dying from radiation sickness in an emergency hospital near Barrie, with scores of people already dead. The scale of the calamity was too big to be true.

She sat up and got out of bed, intending to have a quiet smoke in the kitchen. She put on a quilted blue robe trimmed with white lace—another bonus from Morris Weinstein—and wrapped it around her. In her rush to pack she'd forgotten to take slippers, and she pushed her feet into the high-heeled shoes under the bunk. They clip-clopped on the bare boards, but she didn't care about the noise. Gray blankets had been nailed over the rear windows of the hall: something that had been added while she slept. Curious to see the reason for the blackout, she hurried to the window, pulled back the covering, and recoiled in horror.

The barn doors were wide apart and the interior was ablaze with light from portable floodlights hooked up to trailing cables. Inside, the bunks were filled with people, two in each bunk. Even as her mouth flew open men carried more stretchers over the threshold and rolled the occupants into the empty bunks. She knew they were dead.

The men worked silently, like Styxian boatmen, ferrying the dead from trucks which had quietly drawn into the schoolyard in the moonless night. They were using the barn as a transfer place, awaiting official word on how—and where—to dispose of the bodies. Soon orders would come through for a communal burial. EMO officials were slitting open and checking the contents of paper bags attached to the victims' clothing —personal possessions and papers. They then scribbled names and addresses in thick ledger books.

Rita whirled around, but the grisly sight drew her head slowly back as if it were a magnet. It *was* true, then. The ambulance attendant had not been lying. These people had died from radiation, but they must have been directly in the path of the first intensively radioactive air currents that blew from the station. She'd be all right, despite her reluctance to leave when the alarms first sounded. Her place was well north of the stream of contaminated air, and she'd left before the wind had fanned it out. She ran her fingertips over her face with a delicate movement and brushed her hair back, patting it reassuringly.

"That's it," the man who appeared to be in charge in the barn called out gruffly. He waved his arms to indicate that he wanted the big doors closed and two of the men put their shoulders to the wooden plank doors and slid them together. Another man appeared directly under where she stood, coiling the electric cable around his hand and elbow. A hurried conference was held, the men gathering on the planked roadway in front of the barn. The EMO official said something to one of the men, and he disappeared. She heard a vehicle door close. He reappeared, carrying a carpenter's carryall toolbox and a hand drill, went up to the doors, and drilled some holes. Then he took steel fittings and screwed them to the door. A moment later he had secured the doors with a heavy padlock.

The men retired, their footfalls silent in the soft snow, now stirred up by their tracking back and forth with their gruesome loads. As far as Rita could judge, she had been the only witness of the macabre scene. She heard a truck door slam on the side road, and the soft growl of the vehicle as it drove away.

She sat on the kitchen counter, legs swinging, puffing a cigarette. She took a deep draw, and perked her head as a child cried in its sleep, the sound inharmonious with the faint mixture of snores and grunts. The cigarette tasted stale and she stubbed it out and went back to bed, trying not to think of the scene in the barn.

An hour later she fell asleep, and it seemed as if she had just closed her eyes when she awoke as the early light crept into the lofty hall. She turned on her stomach and suddenly felt lonely. If she could just stretch out her arm and encircle Ray's slim body, draw herself to him, and feel his hard, warm flesh as she snuggled against him, the top of her head under his chin. She closed her eyes tightly. When she opened them she could see Shirley Long stretched out in the lower bunk opposite. The girl was startled as she awoke to the still unfamiliar surroundings, and she glanced over to check that her mother was near. She caught Rita's eye, and Rita smiled and stiffly flicked her fingers in greeting, but Shirley looked very solemn, her round eyes filled with interest and then shyness, almost suspicion.

"Hi," Rita whispered. "Sleep okay?"

The girl nodded.

"I wonder what's for breakfast. I'm hungry," Rita said, enunciating her words clearly but offhandedly. Shirley raised her eyebrows.

"You hungry too?"

Shirley nodded again.

"I'm for bacon and two eggs. What say we take a look?"

The girl abruptly stiffened under the bedsheets and turned away. When she looked back at Rita's face her eyes narrowed, but then they dissolved into two saucy globes that held a hint of mischief. Her body relaxed, and her lips curved in a pleasant grin. Rita slipped off the bunk and pulled on her robe, and went to the girl's bunk. Shirley hopped out, and Rita took the dressing gown from the foot of the girl's bed and held it for her. They tiptoed to the kitchen.

Two women from the village were already there, working behind the closed door. Rita put her head around the opening. One of the women said "Good morning" politely and went on with her work. Rita stood halfway in and halfway out. A man came through the outer door carrying a fifty-pound sack of potatoes on his back. "Where d' yer wan' 'em?" he asked the woman in a rough voice. "Over there'll do, Jack," she said, indicating a corner of the big room.

"Can we help?"

"Sure can use some 'elp 'round 'ere," the younger of the women said seriously, "what with that army o' people and kids in there." She tossed her head in the direction of the assembly hall.

"You've just got two helpers," Rita entered the kitchen with Shirley. "We're good at cooking bacon and eggs and things, aren't we, Shirley?" She grinned knowledgeably at the girl, who smiled broadly.

"There's eggs and the bacon in the icebox. But I don't think we've got enough for everybody," the woman said, consulting a list on a clipboard hanging on a cupboard door. "The rest'll 'ave to make do with the 'tators."

Rita surveyed the egg cartons and the bacon in the icebox and told Shirley to take out the meat while she handled the eggs. The girl was pleased to help. Rita allowed herself to be directed by the women. The kitchen was well equipped to handle meals for schoolchildren, and in a few minutes Rita had the bacon sizzling in several frypans on the two stoves. By the time the first people were shuffling around in the hall a score of dishes was ready to be whisked from the kitchen to the trestle tables outside.

"Better get them 'tators goin'," the woman ordered.

"What'll I do—mash them and light brown them?"

"Yeah. Best thing. That'll fill 'em up," she said philosophically.

"Where's your masher?" Rita asked.

The woman pointed to a worn stick that hung by a piece of blackened string on a hook over the stove. "There," she jerked her head. Her hands were up to the elbows in dough for the monster apple pie she was constructing.

133

"That?"

"Yeah—that!"

"I don't see how—"

The woman proved the nature and purpose of the stick by suddenly taking her hands out of the dough, grabbing the piece of wood, and thrusting it into a large pan where potatoes simmered. She attacked them vigorously, stirring and churning until they started to flake into pulp. She gave Rita an intolerant look and sucked in her breath.

Rita said nothing and got on with the job, her back to the two women. Shirley's face appeared at her elbow, and two round eyes looked up. When Rita glanced down Shirley snickered, shaking her shoulders. Rita smiled, sharing a moment of secret understanding.

The door opened and Rosie Long appeared, wrapped in an oversize dressing gown. "Oh, there you are, Shirley. I thought you'd be here."

"Hi, Rosie. Sleep well? We're just getting breakfast ready. You'll have to hurry if you want bacon and eggs," Rita said cheerfully.

"How did you sleep? And you, Shirley?" Rosie added anxiously. Shirley uttered something that sounded like "Hine Muum" and then pointed with delight to the contents of the pot she was stirring with the stick. "Puut—aat—oh!" the utterance came from the roof of her mouth in a series of glottal stops. Rosie stared at Rita's face, searching for some indication of surprise, a flicker of disgust, of pity perhaps, but she failed to find any emotion registered there.

"I'll go and get dressed," Rosie said, and disappeared. Other women came to offer help, and the woman in charge thanked them with rough politeness and organized a waitress squad to carry the dishes of bacon and eggs and the warm potato hash to the tables. Unshaven husbands came in and joined their families at the tables. Rosie Long reappeared at the kitchen door.

"Better get dressed," she said to her daughter.

Shirley looked at Rita. "I think we're all through," Rita said, glancing around at the empty cooking pots. "I'm going to get dressed, too."

The woman in charge of the kitchen stood at the door, propping it open with her ample elbow, and surveyed the scene with satisfaction. Her helper looked over her shoulder. "Went fine, didn't it?" she said in a moanful voice.

"I'm used to feeding them 'undred kids every day, Maggie. All you got is Cliff an' the kids," she replied in a superior manner.

There was a bustle of activity in the assembly hall as the women set about making beds and tidying up. Rita thought about the charnel house behind the school building and wondered if she was still the only person privy to its secret. She frowned as she tried to smooth out the creases in her gold evening dress, and carefully laid it on the bed. She'd locked the fur cape in the locker under the bunk, and checked it to see that it wasn't being crushed by the weight of the other clothes she'd piled on top.

What if some kids found a way into the barn? She knew what kids are like, they'd find a way into anything. There were bound to be some loose boards somewhere. She glanced up. The rear windows were still covered with the blankets. As she looked a man walked past, curiously lifted a corner and peered out.

She heard a sudden intake of breath at her shoulder. Shirley was looking at the gold dress with open admiration, her hands in front of her body, palms outward.

"Do you like it?" Rita asked, turning so that the girl could see her lips. Shirley nodded energetically, struggling to enunciate her sense of wonder. She'd never seen such sparkle from a dress before. It scintillated with a light of its own.

"It—it's—bewh—bewh—"

Rita looked casually at the girl's face.

"Bewh—ti—ti . . ."

Rita drew the dress toward her and placed the lustrous cloth in the girl's hands. Shirley fingered it delicately.

"—ti—ful," Shirley concluded. Her mouth was open in wonderment, and her eyes shone. She turned to show the dress to her mother, to share her excitement, to make sure she had heard her utter the word completely. But Rosie had gone.

Rita held the dress against Shirley's slim young body. She was almost as tall as Rita. The girl sucked in her breath. "On you it looks good, too!" Rita laughed.

Shirley opened her mouth but words would not come. All she could manage was: "Ahh—ahh—oohd . . ."

"Yes—it's yours!" Rita exclaimed with a flush of generosity. "But it's going to need some alterations. I know someone who can fix it up." In her line of business she knew many tailors who did excellent recutting jobs.

Shirley suddenly threw her arms around Rita and kissed her warmly. Rita could hear a deep rumbling in the girl's throat. She felt the firm cheek and smelled the evanescent sweetness of youth, and was filled with remembrance of things long past. When she spoke she wasn't sure she could trust her voice.

"You're welcome," she said, and turned away. She stuffed the lacy black underwear out of sight in the flight bag and zippered it up.

Rosie returned. Shirley held up the dress and with one hand pointed in deaf-mute language to Rita, to the dress, and to herself.

"Oh—you shouldn't have," Rosie said to Rita loudly. She didn't want Rita to get the impression that she couldn't afford to dress her child properly. She examined the gown closely. "It's too good to give away. I mean—"

"I'm in the business," Rita said offhandedly. "It's okay. Don't worry about it. Honest, dear. She fell in love with it." She spoke with affection for the girl, and turned her face so that Shirley could read her lips.

"It's very good of you. But I'll have to alter it. It'll need pulling in around the bodice and—"

"I know someone who'll do it for me—for nothing," Rita said. "As soon as we get back to the city I'll take it in. You'll see, this guy'll make it look as though it was made for her," she added knowledgeably.

As far as she was concerned the matter was closed. She finished tidying up her things, turned the key in the locker, and sat on the edge of the bed. The family that had moved in next to them was discussing where they could go for a walk. One of the boys suggested to his brother that they explore the school grounds. Rita was relieved to see some EMO men enter the hall and look around; they'd make sure nobody went near the barn.

"What about a drive into the village, Rosie?"

"That'll be nice. Can't see nothing much to do 'anging round here."

Her car was no longer blocked in. It started easily, and within a few minutes they were moving slowly down the frozen side road, with Shirley in the front bucket seat and Rosie in the back. A cigarette hung from Rita's mouth, the filter tip stained scarlet.

There were few people about in the village street, evacuees and a couple of farmer-looking men with EMO armbands. She drove to the other end of the street and headed toward the highway.

"Let's go for a ride, Rosie. There's nothing else to do." She switched on the radio in time to hear an announcer saying: "This is the Emergency Measures Organization's official station. Here is a repeat of the earlier announcement about radiation hazards. If you suspect that you have been exposed to radiation, report to the medical ward at any of the reception centers. Symptoms of radiation exposure include vomiting, nausea, or diarrhea. If none of these symptoms is evident but excessive loose hair appears on your comb, report this to the doctor."

The radio fell silent and crackled as the car passed under high-tension cables. Rita reached out to turn it off, but her hand stayed poised on the knob, undecided.

"Latest report from the Fairfield Nuclear Power Station is that all operating personnel left safely after the plant was abandoned. All workers in the station left in an orderly fashion. There was no panic. Engineers in charge of the station were airlifted to EMO control headquarters at Aurora, north of Toronto, where they are now in consultation with scientists from the Atomic Energy Control Board flown in from Ottawa."

Rita braked at the Stop sign and turned on to the highway. "Looks like they've got everything under control," Rosie said.

"Sounds like it," Rita replied. Ray was safe, then. They were probably grilling him right now, asking all sorts of questions about why the accident happened. They might even blame him. That would be carrying it too far—they couldn't blame one man for wrecking a huge, inanimate power station, even if it had affected so many people, hundreds of thousands of people, two million. No. It would have been the aftershock from the earthquake. She'd heard the radio report about it. She fought to bring her imagination under control. She put out her cigarette in the ashtray and noticed that Shirley had fallen asleep, her head propped sideways on the curved leather seat. She turned off the radio.

"She's dropped off," Rita said quietly to Rosie. "There's a little cushion in the corner where you are. Put it under her cheek."

Rosie eased the cushion into position, and the girl stirred contentedly.

"She's cute. Guess she needs the rest," Rita said.

Rosie stared out of the window. The fields were turning from white to light brown as the snow melted under the fine sunny sky. Rita wondered about Rosie. In the brief period that she had known her, shared almost the some bed, Rosie had been evasive. She wondered about her husband—if there was one—and why Rosie was so tight-lipped about Shirley's affliction. Partly to satisfy her curiosity and partly to relieve the awkward silence, she decided to ask. What the heck, it was no skin off her nose if Rosie didn't want to talk, but she didn't have to be so secretive.

"You two all alone, then?" she said in an even voice.

"Yeah," said Rosie slowly, and Rita could see her face in the rear-view mirror, her lips tight. They were cruising easily, as there was no traffic. They passed a convoy of five food trucks heading in the opposite direction. Rosie felt the silence pressing in. She suddenly felt confined with this bright young woman and the sleeping girl in the small car whirling along the highway.

"My husband left me. It's a long time now," she heard herself saying.

It was Rita's turn to be silent. She hadn't suspected that less than a dozen words could have the power to make her want to bite off her tongue. Shut up, you idiot, she told herself. You had to open your big mouth.

"I'm sorry," she said quietly, and glanced around for an instant to look directly at Rosie. "She's such a nice kid."

"He was a bum. No use wasting sympathy on him," Rosie said, her eyes dull.

Rita shook her head uncertainly. Again she wished she hadn't asked the question. Rosie began to loosen up as the bitter memories flooded back.

"He was a plumber—doing good at it, too, with his own business. But he had the moneybug," she continued. "He'd always wanted a boy, never took any interest in her." She nodded toward the front seat. "I brought her up on my own. I took him to court, but it's a man's world and I didn't get much of an allowance. Since the divorce came through I got a bit more for a while. But you can't bring up a 'andicapped kid and try to live like anything decent on a pittance. He went bankrupt. He was rotten right through," she said in a thin voice, and sank back in the corner.

Rita lit another cigarette. She rolled down the window a bit.

"I 'aven't 'eard 'ide nor 'air about him for seven years now," Rosie said. It had been many years since she'd allowed herself the gratification of voicing her self pity. "It wasn't like he was knocking around with another woman—I'd 'ave forgiven him for that. He was just plain callous, didn't 'ave much feeling for her when she was a baby." She leaned forward until her chin rested on the back of the front seat.

"Do you get anything—money, I mean—from him now?"

"Not a dime. I support myself and Shirley from my own wages. I wouldn't take a penny from him now anyways, not the way he treated her." Again she nodded at the sleeping girl. "And I paid for my 'ouse with every penny from my own earnings. It's all paid for, even though it's down near Cabbagetown. It's a good clean place. And them people are decent, clean-living people. I got some good neighbors."

Rita said: "Do you have a good job, Rosie?"

"I work for myself. Cleaning lady," she stated with a touch of pride. "In my spare time I do a bit of dressmaking. That's 'ow I know there's a lot of work in altering that lovely gold dress. Really, you shouldn't 'ave given it to her like that. It's a very expensive dress." She drummed her fingers on the top of the upholstery, fingers with broken, scarred nails and callouses on the thumbs from holding brooms and mop handles.

"Can you cut out suits and things like that?"

"Sure. When Shirl was a baby I used to make all her clothes." She warmed to her topic and glowed pleasantly with the memory. "You ought to have seen her in the little pleated skirt-and-jacket outfit I made when she was three. Everybody used to turn around and stare. 'Isn't she cute!' they'd say when me an' George used to take her for a walk on Sundays. But that was before we found out she'd be deaf and dumb for life." Her voice dropped and trailed away. She flopped back in the seat.

"Is it really permanent? How do you know?"

"We had specialists. They shook their 'eads after they examined her."

"But she spoke to me this morning—she understands what I say," Rita said.

"She spoke—to you? You must be mistaken. She's never said more'n a part of a word or two to anybody—ever. She says something to me now and again—animal sounds like you heard in the kitchen. But I know she reads your lips 'cos you speak very distinct like. But speak to anybody? Oh, never."

"But she did," Rita exclaimed emphatically, turning around to face Rosie momentarily. She said 'It's beautiful' when I gave her the dress."

"She said that? You understood?" She spoke in measured tones as realization turned slowly to faint hope born of a long-suppressed yearning.

"I understood her perfectly. She stuttered when she said them, but that's what she came out with—'It's beautiful' clear as a bell!"

"Those doctors can't all be wrong," Rosie said doubtfully. "And the ones at the school—she goes to the School for the Deaf in Toronto. That's how she knows her three Rs and all that. She's quite bright, really. Came fourth from the top last term," she added pridefully.

"You know, Rosie, I'm a bit of a gambler myself—at least that's what my friends say about me," Rita laughed, thinking of the buyers from other fashion houses, and Rosie smiled, comforted in some strange way by this forthright young woman with the headstrong manner and the generous heart. "I'm willing to bet ten to one that by the time Shirley's twenty and looking around for some lucky guy to marry she'll be speaking as good as you or I."

It sounded so good! Just to hear Rita speak. But it was too good to be true. If only it would ever come true, Rosie thought, sighing deeply. She had a vision of Shirley grown up, going on dates, perhaps in a smart sports car like this, with the roof down and her hair streaming in the wind, like the television commercials. And there'd be a boy, of course, behind the wheel with dark hair and a scarf carelessly thrown around his neck. And he'd be smiling—smiling with his head half turned toward her Shirl. And she'd be telling him to keep his eyes on the road. Telling him, and listening to the music of the car radio, and hearing the wind rushing past. Oh God, if only . . . if only . . . She wiped the tears away with a crumpled handerchief. She swallowed and sank again into the corner. The rich upholstery felt snug and consoling, and she longed to close her eyes and fall asleep, to dream of Shirley with her boy friend.

The car slowed. "What's this?" Rita said loudly, peering ahead. "It looks like a roadblock." Rosie sat up, her wonderful world of make-believe dissolving. Rita pulled up as a man with an EMO armband hurried from a sentrylike box at the side of the road and barred the way with his upraised hand. He came around to the window.

"Sorry, miss, there's no thoroughfare for civilian cars unless you've got a pass," he said with an air of newly acquired authority.

"Why?" Rita's voice expressed the right degree of demand while remaining on the safe side of courtesy.

"The highway's being used by military trucks and EMO vehicles, miss. We've got strict instructions," he said. "Matter o' fact, you're not supposed to be on this section of the highway, in any case. How'd you get on?"

"Just drove on—like anybody else."

"Funny," the man said, scratching his head. He was ruddy-faced and looked as though he'd spent all his life out of doors. A farmer doing EMO work on a volunteer basis, Rita had decided. He looked down the road from the direction they'd come, then shouted to a man she hadn't noticed in the sentry box: "Hi, Ed, what's the quickest way back south?"

Ed popped his head out of the box, saw Rita's face at the open window, and decided he should investigate matters at closer range.

"What's goin' on 'ere? You're off bounds, miss," he said, running his eyes over the thighs exposed by her short skirt. "EMO's closed all 'ighways 'round 'ere. You'll 'ave to go back south in the other lane. You can cross over the boulevard 'ere." He pointed to the muddy trough where some heavy vehicles had left deep tire tracks in the frozen muck.

Rita smiled at him, and his expression softened. "How far are we from Barrie?" she asked.

" 'Bout twenty-three miles—eh, 'bout that."

"We were thinking of turning back but couldn't find an overpass or cloverleaf. What's that up there?" She pointed to a bridge that spanned the road about a quarter mile ahead.

"Oh, you can't take that road—that's to 'Ighway 27—and it's out of bounds, too." He shook his head seriously, and looked down at her legs again.

She flashed another smile at him, and he was even more impressed. "I was thinking of turning around there and coming south on the other lane. Save going through all that muck there." She tossed her head sideways and her hair fell over her eye. She brushed it back with a deliberate feminine stroke of her black-gloved hand.

"I guess there's no 'arm, miss," the man said hesitantly. "Okay," he added firmly, raising his head for a final look inside the car.

Rita put the car in drive. When she came to the cloverleaf she slewed the wheel around, zipped across the bridge, and sped down the ramp leading to the highway south. There was no traffic, and she pressed the accelerator down firmly. She flashed past the sentry box without even glancing at it, but if she had she would have seen two friendly hands waving at her.

"Well, look who's woken up!" she exclaimed as Shirley yawned and opened her eyes.

In the village main street Rita stopped at a corner store. "Want to see if they've got any newspapers," she told Rosie. "I won't be a minute. Need anything?"

"Thanks. I don't think so."

The only available newspaper was the local one. Rita stared at the screaming three inch deep headline: DEAD AND DYING

EPICENTER

COUNTED IN THOUSANDS. "Ottawa Help Too Late for Many—What Happened?," the subhead questioned.

She stood reading in the middle of the rundown store: "An estimated 30,000 dead and fatally contaminated victims of the Fairfield accident are reported by a reliable source.

"Temporary morgues set up at four of the reception areas north of Toronto are filled to capacity, and relatives are crowding into them seeking lost members of families. At the same reception areas fatally poisoned victims are freezing due to poor heating systems and insufficient blankets. Doctors and nurses are struggling under chaotic conditions.

"If these conditions last another week, or even a few more days, a serious threat of infectious disease hangs over the area. Many victims are already suffering from the flu.

"Aid has been rushed by the International Red Cross from the United States, Britain, France, and other countries. But clearly it is a case of too little too late, and in some cases to the wrong place. A truckful of blankets ended up in an abandoned farmhouse near Gravenhurst, for example, at least forty miles from the nearest reception area.

"Disposal of the dead is a terrible problem. Huge communal graves have been bulldozed in the frozen ground near Barrie and truckloads of corpses are being piled into them daily."

Rita sucked in her breath and read the lead editorial:

"The biggest question everybody is asking remains unanswered. Who boobed by allowing a nuclear power station to be located so near to a big urban area? So far—only questions in Parliament.

"When can we expect Ottawa to make an official announcement when a public enquiry on this national disaster will commence? So far no word from Parliament Hill.

"Another question being asked: Has anybody bothered to check the design of other nuclear stations—and those under

145

construction—to see if they are safe in case another earth-quake occurs?"

She flipped back the pages and read the black-ruled box she'd missed on page one: "The Prime Minister has called for a national day of mourning to take place next Sunday. Churches and synagogues will hold special memorial services for the dead and a two-minute silence will be observed. The Prime Minister will lead the nation in prayer in a service to be held on Parliament Hill at 11:00 A.M."

She folded the newspaper and stuffed it under her coat. "They sold right out," she told Rosie Long as she got back into the car.

NINE

Deighton sat at the center of the long T-shaped conference table, calmly surveying the two dozen faces in the room and twirling the ends of his mustache between lean fingers. The Aurora EMO headquarters had become the official center for battling the disaster that had stricken the city twenty miles south, and he was chairman of the meeting that was about to begin, a meeting of nuclear experts. There was only one item on the agenda: how to stop the radioactive airborne materials from the Fairfield Nuclear Power Station.

The easterly wind had blown the deadly effluent over Toronto for three days and nights, turning the 250 square miles of heavily built-up area—houses, office buildings, factories, expressways, tree-lined streets, and the harbor—into a ghost city. After dark, lights still shone from deserted office buildings, plush hotels, and neon-faced cocktail lounges, and the brightly illuminated windows of downtown stores still displayed the latest fashions to empty silent sidewalks. Nothing stirred in the vast open plaza in front of the modernistic city hall. The only movement came from a flag that flapped limply at the top of a tall metal mast. At night the concave inner surfaces of the twin office towers were brilliantly lighted: tier after tier of blue-lit windows shone in spectral loneliness.

Phantom subway trains were neatly parked at the northern terminus of the main subway line, red and silver coaches that had deposited tens of thousands of harried passengers in front of waiting buses for the slow ride into the countryside.

In the heart of the commercial district the pigons soared and tumbled around the lofty entablatures that decorated the Victorian office buildings on narrow Bay Street, where the financial wheeler-dealers had watched the stock tickers and huddled in dollar-conniving groups. Soon the white and speckled birds would falter and flutter in agony, victims of the radioactive rays now penetrating with icy fingers of death from a clear sky. Occasionally an airplane, carrying sensitive recorders used by the United States Air Force to monitor the fallout over the Pacific from atomic tests made by the Chinese, flew high over the city, tracking the path of the contamination and reporting by radio to Aurora headquarters. The United States Atomic Energy Commission had sent experts to Aurora, and the President had personally telephoned the Prime Minister in Ottawa to pledge every possible assistance.

Deighton rose and looked around the room for a full minute before speaking, easing the cramped quarters into silence. One or two men hastily settled themselves at the end of the table, where Johnson sat with Townsend.

"Gentlemen, let's proceed. The purpose of this meeting is to seek an effective and rapid solution to the problem at Fairfield. Before we begin I'll introduce the gentleman on my right, Major General Howell Parker Waring." A stern-looking man whose iron-gray eyes flashed from a rock-hard face lifted his chin almost imperceptibly. "I'd also like to introduce," Deighton went on, looking to his left, "Mr. Graham D.

EPICENTER

Rheinheimer, director of the Radiation and Biological Division of the United States Department of Health."

The two men acknowledged Deighton's introduction, and he glanced down at the neatly squared papers on the desk.

"If you'll look in the folders in front of you, you'll see some information on Fairfield." There was a shuffle of papers as the men around the table fingered the documents. "At the back you'll find some suggested schemes for coming to grips with the problem."

He paused to allow them to become familiar with the contents of the folders. Johnson unfolded a large blueprint he found in the back of the folder and spread it on the table. He studied it intently, his dark hair glistening as he bent over the stiff paper.

"The schemes for Fairfield are divided into two broad groups—those that propose isolating the source of the contamination by covering the fuel bundles in some way, and those that suggest removing them entirely from the station. Now turn to Scheme One," Deighton continued, his voice more commanding than suggestive. "This is a proposal to build a lead-lined sheath around the bundles and the broken concrete shielding, and it includes a domed roof. Can we have some expression of opinion on this idea?"

The men concentrated on the diagram of the station. A circular structure was indicated by a heavy line around the spot where the fuel bundles lay, and a column of figures down the side of the diagram gave the estimated strength of the radiation.

"I don't see any point in trying to contain the contamination source at the station site. It'll spell trouble later," said a broad beefy man with a ruddy complexion near the head of the table. "It would be like covering a blind boil on your neck

149

hoping it'll go away," he said bluntly. "Much better to get rid of the thing once and for all. In any case, it's too damned hot to get near!"

"I agree," said a youngish man near Johnson. "There's no suit that would give adequate protection for the radiation values shown here." He stabbed with a ballpoint at the paper before him.

Deighton nodded to a bearded man who had raised his hand.

"Scheme Two suggests flooding the bundle area after building a dike around it. I was wondering whether this idea could be carried a step further: build the dike, flood the area, and then pass a shielded flask over each bundle—the same way as bundles are removed from the station's waste-water tank," he said brightly.

Deighton looked thoughtfully at the end of his pencil. It was an appealing idea. From the practical point of view there were no difficult problems to solve. A bridge could be built over the flooded bundles and the flask lowered by remote control. But there was a major snag, which Johnson was quick to point out.

"You'd first have to fish for the bundles underwater and line them up before you could lower the flask over them," he explained.

"Scheme Three for shoving the bundles away by shielded earth-moving machines might be all right for a small amount of contamination, but not for the mess at Fairfield," Townsend said.

"You must get those bundles out of the station! It's the very first consideration!" Waring's voice burst with stentorian volume through the room. He'd jumped to his feet and pulled off the heavy black-rimmed reading glasses he'd put on. He slowly lowered himself into his chair again, glowering over his black frames at Deighton, who looked down at the end of the table.

"Any more comments, gentlemen?" Deighton asked quietly. "Or opinions?"

"This idea of clamping a shielded dome structure over the bundles seems logical," the beefy man spoke up again. "If we could develop some way to put a dome on wheels, the bundles could be wheeled away from the site."

"We wouldn't be able to clear away the ground immediately under the dome—that's highly radioactive, too," Deighton explained. It was obvious that the man knew nothing about civil engineering and had no appreciation of the size of the required structure. "Perhaps our American guest would like to make some comments while people get their back burners thinking on other lines," he added. He looked directly at Rheinheimer. A second later Rheinheimer lumbered to his feet, pushing his chair back. He was a big man, and wore a light gray suit with a small red carnation in the buttonhole. He smiled amiably at Deighton and turned to the attentive faces in the room.

"I'll be frank with you fellas. Anything we can do to help you get Fairfield back into working order we will do— whether it's technical help or supplies you need," he said without condescension. "But from our own point of view, the official United States' view, we are very concerned about the possibility of contamination spreading over to our side of Lake Ontario if the wind shifts around. I received a telegram from the director of the Great Lakes International Joint Commission before I entered this room. He emphasizes the gravity of the situation. Everybody in this room appreciates that fact. We know that Toronto is in one hell of a mess and that your people are suffering, but we are very worried about the possibility of cities in upper New York State getting a dose of contaminated air. Frankly, we're also worried about the stuff falling into the lake near the water-supply intakes of cities on the south shore—"

"We're coming to that—" Deighton snapped, twitching his straggly mustache.

"Then why don't you divide this meeting into two groups —one to decide on the Fairfield problem and another to deal immediately with what to do if the wind swings around?"

Rheinheimer pulled up the chair and sat down, staring at the papers on the table.

"With due respect to our colleague from south of the border, I can't agree to splitting up this meeting," Deighton said crisply. "All the problems are related, and we have assembled here some of the best brains in all fields of nuclear energy." He heard one or two men near the head of the table say "hear, hear" softly, and, reassured by the implied support, continued: "This is an interdisciplinary group. An idea from one can spawn an idea in another."

Feet shuffled, and a murmur arose round the table. Rheinheimer was the focal point for cool glances from the far end of the table, where a sprinkling of younger men was seated.

"Let's get on as fast as possible with the order of business, which is Fairfield!" Waring roared, thumping the agenda sheet with his fist. Deighton seized the chance to put his view forward.

"We've discussed methods but we've not had any conclusive opinion on whether the better way is to get rid of the contamination source bodily or seal it up on the spot," he exclaimed. "I'm in favor of getting it away."

"Let's have a show of hands on it," someone suggested from the back of the room.

"All in favor of moving the bundles right out of Fairfield," Deighton called, raising his chin to count. A wave of hands appeared around the table.

"We're in agreement after all," he said, casting a fast look in Rheinheimer's direction. "Now," he paused significantly, and added: "How?"

"The main trouble with a shielded cover over the bundles is the weight," said Johnson. "We must first develop a means to shield the radioactivity so that we can safely approach the bundles, and then think of a method of transporting the whole damned thing from the site—including the ground immediately under and around the bundles. We must know what the surface of the ground is made of. I can't see any specification for it in this material." He thumbed through the papers and looked up.

"Four inches of standard paving asphalt on a rubble base nine inches thick," Deighton replied succinctly. Johnson looked up and smiled. "So we'll need to dig down at least three feet," Deighton went on. He'd taken a small slide rule from his breast pocket and made a quick calculation.

"That would put it on the safe side," Johnson agreed.

"This, then, is the requirement," Deighton said with a note of finality. "A shield to contain the radioactivity. It must be transportable and must remove the source of the contamination plus the ground on which it stands down to a depth of three feet." The others around the table wrote it down. He read it out loud to make sure everybody had it right.

"The shielding is easy, but heavy. Any ideas on a light-weight shielding?" he asked.

Johnson glanced up. He'd been studying the papers while Deighton spoke. "There's no substitute for lead to shield gamma rays. We all agree on that, I think," he said.

EPICENTER

"What about dense concrete?" someone asked.

"It would have to be much thicker than lead, and we'd be up against the weight again," Johnson replied.

Deighton nodded. "Assume we use lead, what about transportation?" he asked, looking around the table for an answer.

The room fell silent. Johnson found the atmosphere oppressive, despite the air conditioning, and his attention began to wander. Through the partly opened door connecting the conference room with the main switchboard room he could see EMO officials scribbling reports as messages flooded in by radio-telephone from the monitoring planes and mobile patrols. The reports, when they were coordinated, presented a dismal picture of the misery that had descended on the metropolitan area. The wind had freshened on the third day, blowing the radioactive plumes from the vent discharge stacks on the Fairfield station roof in a steady stream downwind. As the hours wore on the discharge developed into a coning pattern, spreading rapidly downward and sideways. The invisible cloud had swept through the downtown area and into the western suburbs. In the countryside, the radioactive level had diminished but the monitoring equipment at Toronto International Airport, west of the city, registered danger, and all flying operations had ceased two days earlier. Air Canada was bringing its intercity jets into the London, Ontario, airport about a hundred miles west, and overseas and transcontinental flights, including New York traffic, were being rerouted to Montreal.

In the smaller cities and towns that lay around the sprawling city, people waited for the latest news of the direction and strength of the contamination. The Canadian Broadcasting Corporation had assumed all broadcasting responsibility in the area and taken over operation of the private television and radio stations. Prerecorded tapes broadcast survival instructions, and flash news reports gave the latest position of the plumes and of suspected contaminated areas.

By the afternoon of the first day most of the metropolitan area had been evacuated. EMO director Ferrisston, sitting silently at General Waring's elbow, had tucked into his briefcase the latest report on the estimated number of casualties. In the reception areas the public buildings and hurriedly assembled portable hospitals were jammed with people. Anyone suspected of radiation exposure after being tested with a dosimeter had been hastily segregated and packed into special wards. The EMO officials on duty tried to separate the men from the women and children. This had seemed effective on paper, but husbands refused to be separated and pushed in after their families as they were led to bunk beds in the primitive rooms.

At a reception center near Barrie an officious EMO man ordered a young husband to leave his pregnant wife, a girl in her twenties. During the erratic drive north her labor pains had begun.

"You'd better wait outside," the official with the EMO armband ordered gruffly.

"I'm coming in!" the young man yelled.

"I've strict instructions—women only!"

"But my wife—can't you see?" the husband shouted, his voice angry and frightened.

"It's orders. You can't come in!" the man said obstinately, putting his hand firmly on the husband's shoulder. The next second the official was sprawled on his back in the snow.

"I'll get you for that!" he roared at the husband, who was helping his wife across the threshold. A woman called, "Don't be stupid—can't you see her condition?"

Nobody made any attempt to restrain the EMO man as he rushed into the doorway after the husband and swung his fist at the younger man. He missed and hit the wife in the chest. The husband grabbed a stubby piece of scaffolding pipe from the floor and brought it down with all his strength on the EMO man's head. A Red Cross nurse rushed to him and bent over, felt his pulse, and peered into his eye. "Dead!" she said, and looked accusingly at the young man. His wife screamed, gagged her mouth with her hand, and drew back in terror. They led her away while two EMO officials took the struggling husband to a police hut that had been erected on the site.

Medical attendants classified people they thought had been contaminated as casualties and herded them into portable hospitals. There they ordered them to undress and get rid of contaminated clothing, and told them to shower in canvas booths. The water was cold, but most people took the showers and scrubbed their bodies when they understood that their skins might be affected. Some people refused to undress because many of the heating systems had not been connected and the rooms were frigidly cold. At the entrance to each building a Red Cross official laboriously wrote down the name, sex, address, and age of the casualties as they entered, to help relatives or friends trace missing people. In a hospital near Uxbridge a father, mother, and four small children arrived inside the back of a Remedial Evacuation truck. Their oldest son, a boy of fifteen, had been at a party at the other end of the city the night of the disaster, and they had not seen him since.

"He'd have gone back home, I'm sure," the woman cried to the nurse who smoothed her bedcovers. "He must still be there. Can't someone go for him?"

"We've given his name and address to the EMO men. They'll do their best to find him," the nurse tried to calm the woman. "Here's the doctor."

The doctor examined the woman's fine dark hair, then

looked into her eyes with his small focusing flashlight. His lips dropped at the corners. "Where're the children?" he asked. He seemed to know about the family. The nurse pointed to a double bunk into which the four children had been squeezed. He examined the youngest child, a girl about a year old, who cried when she was picked up. The doctor whispered something to the nurse, put the baby down, and looked at the other children, ranging in age from three to seven. Each time he examined a child he spoke quietly to the nurse about radio-iodine ingestion. The mother strained to hear.

"Where's your husband?" the doctor asked kindly, but his voice conveyed concern.

"In the men's ward—they wouldn't let us stay together," she replied, and started to cry.

"The nurse will take care of you. I'll go and see your husband now and tell him you're being taken care of." He gave the nurse a meaningful look.

The next day the woman's fine dark hair began to fall from her scalp, and the skin on the baby's face turned a mottled red. The other children complained of diarrhea, and they retched after eating the plain hospital food.

Ferrisston had quietly studied the reports before passing them to General Waring. The men around the table were officially unaware of the dreadful details because Waring had purposely kept them uninformed, not wanting them to have to bear the additional strain that knowledge would bring.

Deighton suddenly rose and drew the outline of a huge dome on the blackboard. The noise of his chair scraping on the wooden floor brought Johnson's attention back to the problem.

"I remember a new type of earth-boring machine that the National Research Council designed for a mining company in

Quebec," Deighton said thoughtfully, stroking his mustache and leaving a wide chalk slash across his chin. "It had heavy knives that rotated under the rim and folded back to grasp the earth." He made a gripping motion with his right hand. "I wonder if anybody's heard about it? We might try to adapt the idea to dig around the fuel bundles."

"Hey—I remember that rig," the red-faced man called out. "They pulled me in on it for the electrics. It might work. The knives were driven by an electric motor."

An aide entered and rushed to General Waring, who glanced up over his glasses. The ruddy man lumbered on, recalling the electrical details of the earth-drilling machine as the aide handed a sheet of paper to the general. Waring read the latest meteorological report, the rolls of muscle around the corners of his mouth tightening. He coughed loudly to attract Deighton's attention, and Deighton waved to the man to stop talking.

"Here's the latest met report from low-altitude radiosonde balloons we released over Fairfield early this morning," Waring said gruffly. "The easterly wind veered to the south about two hours ago and has since died. At the moment the air is static over the power station—no wind."

The men around the table seemed to relax collectively, and one or two smiled. They jumped when Rheinheimer's fist hit the table. "If it veered south before dying that means it could swing to the northwest when it starts up. Then we'd get the fallout in New York State!" he yelled.

"Not necessarily," Deighton replied quietly. "It could stay southerly and blow north—right up here, as a matter of fact."

"You don't know, and I don't know," Rheinheimer shouted across the table, pointing his pudgy finger aggressively. "It's anyone's guess. But everybody here knows the prevailing wind is from the northwest at this time of year."

EPICENTER

"Which is all the more reason we should quit arguing and get on with clearing those damned bundles out!" Waring roared, his face screwed into angry lines.

"Gentlemen! Gentlemen!" Deighton cried, rising. "We're all overtired and have desperate problems, but please, lets keep this meeting on a civilized level." He looked around the room. "Mr. Rheinheimer is here to give us the benefit of his experience on the biological effects of radiation—and God knows we're going to need all the help we can get. He's right about a change in wind direction. It's something the EMO and we have to consider. If the wind changes, all our problems are going to be multiplied."

The room quieted down. Deighton turned to General Waring. "Have you got other balloons monitoring the wind direction, sir?"

"We're sending them up every half hour and using radar to track them since the wind dropped. As soon as there's a change in wind direction the balloons will show it and I'll get a radio report to you immediately."

"Thank you, sir. We'll carry on with our plans to get those bundles away . . ."

TEN

The MacGregors settled uneasily into the farmhouse they'd been sent to by the EMO evacuee center in Barrie. The farm was seven miles from the town, near the shore of Lake Simcoe. From the little room Alice MacGregor shared with Pamela she could see that the early spring ice had started to thaw in the center of the twenty-mile-wide lake, and here and there the sun glinted on the open water, blue under the clear sky. Andy had been given a small room on the ground floor next to the living room. Agnes Wellington, their landlady, was a widow, and her son Percival worked the eighty-acre farm in summer and supplemented his meager earnings as a builder's laborer in town. Percival was a bachelor in his late forties, and at the moment was showing Pamela how to clear the stuck clothesline strung across the backyard of the old farmhouse.

"Give this pulley a shove—so—and the line'll be free. Just like this!" He yanked the frayed galvanized wire and pulled it from the pulley bracket. "There, now she's okay."

Pamela thanked him and lifted the laundry piece by piece on to the line. She and her mother had spent the whole morning washing their clothes by hand in the cement laundry tubs in the basement. Mrs. Wellington couldn't afford a washing machine; her only electrical appliances were an old stove and a small refrigerator, and lately that had been giving trouble. There was no television set, but she had a radio in the living room, an old tube set in a battered walnut cabinet that was a source of curiosity to Andy, coming as he did from a world of transistorized radios in streamlined plastic cases. When the novelty of life on the farm began to diminish after the third day, he said he missed television.

"You'll just have to wait till you get home," his mother said bluntly. "Can't you find something to help Mr. Wellington with?"

"He's gone into town."

"Maybe Mrs. Wellington needs something done."

Andy sighed and went out into the back of the farmhouse. The land fell in a gentle slope down to a wide bay with summer cottages here and there along the shore. He could see the smoke rising from the stovepipe chimneys, blue against the lifeless brown trees on the other side of the bay. All the city people who owned lakeside cottages were now in them and were installing wood stoves. The Barrie hardware merchants and builders' suppliers had sold every stove in stock during the first day of the evacuation, and electric heaters had gone the same way. The linen stores were sold out of blankets and sheets, and there had been a rush on food stores.

The EMO supplies branch had gone into full-scale operation. Caches of preserved food, blankets, and utility clothing were opened, and depots were organized in Barrie and other reception areas. But it was the volunteer help that came from other parts of Canada and from the United States that made it possible for life to be sustained with any degree of comfort. Trucks laden with canned food, warm clothing, and blankets thundered down the Trans-Canada Highway from Winnipeg, more than a thousand miles away. Centers to receive these supplies had been opened in downtown Winnipeg and people came from miles around to deposit food, bottles of pop, preserved meat, and thousands of garments of every description. Supplies had poured in from cities in southern Ontario, and trains as far away as Vancouver and Calgary were being loaded with essential materials to sustain a displaced population of two million people. Trains arriving from Montreal were loaded with medical supplies, drugs, and portable hospitals complete with modern operating rooms and mobile stations for generating electricity. They also carried volunteer doctors and nurses.

The smoke across the bay drifted straight up in the windless sky and dispersed. Farther away, to the north, Andy could see the contrail of a high-flying jet. He looked intently at the front of the slender plume, but the plane was too far away for him to see. Suddenly Percival Wellington's old car rattled around the corner of the barn and up the long cart track from the road, and Andy ran toward the car as it stopped in front of the house.

"Hi, young 'un," Percival greeted him cheerfully. "Look what I got." He held up two rabbits by their hind legs. "Ever tasted rabbit pie?"

"Nope," Andy said. "What's it taste like?"

"The best," Percival grinned, showing two irregular rows of tobacco-stained teeth.

"Why didn't you tell me you were going shooting? I'd have liked to have come."

"I didn't go shooting. Old Doc Matthews gave them to me. He's the vet down on the third concession road."

A look of suspicion came over Andy's face. "They didn't die of disease did they?"

Wellington laughed and slung the two carcasses over his

shoulder. "No, Doc doesn't cure wild animals. Only sick cows and 'orses like. These are what he shot for sport."

Life in the country was something new for Andy. The far-ranging openness of the snow-covered farmlands gave him a new kind of perspective and helped to push the memory of his father's death into the background. On the fourth day of the evacuation, Wellington took him ice-fishing on the lake. He'd built a little hut that he'd towed on to the ice with his old car and then left there for the winter. They went out on foot and stayed until lunchtime dropping a baited line through a hole that Wellington had chopped in the ice. They each caught one small whiting, which Andy wanted to throw back.

"No—we'll eat 'em!" Wellington cried, before the boy let go of them over the hole. Brought up on the edge of bare sub-sistence, Percival Wellington knew that two small fish could eke out a meal of potatoes and beans. He wrapped them in some broken ice and newspaper. "There. Ma'll cook 'em. They're tasty," he said, jamming shut the rough door of the hut.

Pamela was astonished when she saw the fish Wellington unwrapped on the kitchen table. "Fresh fish in winter!" she exclaimed. "Hey, Mom. Look!"

"Looks like a choice of rabbit pie or fish for supper," Alice MacGregor said. She'd been helping old Mrs. Wellington with the cooking and household chores since they'd arrived, and the preoccupation with work had kept her mind off her grief.

The crude life in the farmhouse dismayed Pamela. She detested the inadequate stove and the inefficient hot-air furnace. The big old two-story house was drafty and the floors cracked ominously when she walked across them. Her grief was still raw, and over everything hung the worry of not knowing where Ken, her fiancé, was. He'd telephoned before the MacGregors struggled north in their old Chevvy; he had to take care of his aged mother and had been bound for an unspecified reception center up north. Pamela listened hourly to the radio broadcasts that listed missing persons and persons sought by others, but Ken's name never came up. It seemed impossible that the happy days of less than three weeks ago had quickly turned into sad hours that dragged through dreary days.

Percival drove into Barrie with Andy on the morning of the fifth day to buy some tea, coffee, and bread. When he turned in at the supermarket parking lot a bored-looking soldier waved him into a space between two other cars. An EMO official rushed up as Percival opened the car door.

"This'll entitle you to ten dollars' worth of food. It's a government ration," the official said sternly, scribbling the license-plate number of Percival's car on a slip of paper. Percival took the slip and looked puzzled. "But I only want some bread and tea and—"

"You can use the slip. But you can't go over ten dollars."

"What's this? Rationing?"

"Just a precautionary measure to conserve food supplies," the official said. He turned and raced to another car.

The line-up in the store extended from the check-out counters, around the store, and back to the entrance. As Percival and Andy approached the entrance a soldier indicated with a wave of his semiautomatic weapon that they were to form another queue just outside the door.

"Blow me down—jest for a loaf o' bread and tea and coffee? Come on, young 'un, we'll take our business to some other place." The soldier showed no emotion as they went back to the car. Percival tossed the slip of paper out of the window.

"Hey—you can't do that! It's a ration for ten dollars' of food!" the EMO man yelled indignantly, rushing to pick up the pink form. "Didn't you hand it in?"

"Nope—didn't buy nothing!"

The man put the form back under an elastic band that kept the pile of slips in place. "Don't you ever throw them away like that again. Somebody'll find it and get two rations' worth of food," he said officiously. Percival spat out of the window.

"Let's go an' see ol' Mallett. He won't 'ave none of this nonsense."

The grocery store around the corner from the main street had been in the Mallett family for three generations, and Percival's mother had taken him there as a little boy to buy the week's supplies. The door was open, and the shelves were completely bare. Percival was too surprised to say anything to Old Man Mallett, who sat behind the scratched counter with a cashbook in his hand. When he recovered Percival said: "Eh? What gives, Elmer? Looks like you sold out 'o everything."

The old man looked up, his face beaming with pleasure. "Ain't seen nothing like this since the last war. Them army fellas came and bought me right out. Looks like Sarah and me'll be goin' to Florida for the rest o' the winter after all." He grinned.

"What the heck does a guy have to do to buy a loaf o' bread around here?" He told the old man about the ration slips at the supermarket. "Next thing you'll know the blasted government will get us all conscripted," he added grimly.

"I'll get Sarah to give yer a loaf," the old man said, and walked unsteadily to the rear of the store where he lived with his wife. He reappeared with a loaf of homemade bread, which he wrapped in an old newspaper and presented to Percival. "They took all my wrapping paper and bags too," he said apologetically.

"Thanks very much," Percival said quietly. "Ma won't believe me when I tell her. This is Andy. He's staying with us with his sister and Ma till they can go back to the city. What d'you think about all this nonsense?"

"That radioactivity stuff? Lots of bull's wool if yer ask me," the old man said. "On the western front we used to stick wet handkerchiefs over our mugs when the Germans let off that green gas. Ain't they got modern gasmasks for all that now?"

Alice MacGregor looked at Percival with utter disbelief when he told her about the rationing.

"It's just like it was during the war when I was a little girl in Glasgow. Who'd have believed—"

"It's true, Mom. This guy came up to us and handed Mr. Wellington this slip, and—"

"Maybe yer ma'll like to rest a bit," Percival interrupted.

Alice MacGregor couldn't sleep that night. She lay in a numbed daze worrying about future food supplies and how much radiation she and her family had absorbed during their rush from the city. She quietly slipped out of bed without disturbing Pamela and sat in a high old-fashioned chair before the window, looking out over the peaceful countryside that lay under a starlit night. In the distance she could see the other side of the lake where it narrowed into a bay. The cottages were dark, but here and there headlights flashed as traffic moved on the highway beyond. It was a calming sight, and the absence of sound helped to clarify her thoughts. Only an occasional creak disturbed the silence as the old wooden house contracted under the cold of the February night.

They had left as soon as the sirens sounded and their house was on the east side of the power station. If the wind had been blowing toward the west, there'd have been nothing dangerous blowing in their direction, she decided. And by the time they'd reached the highway north, they would have been far enough from Fairfield to be out of danger. She thought this over for a while and concluded it was a reasonable judgment.

She shivered, and pulled the robe around her. Ken was a worry. If only they knew where he was, or just knew for certain that he was safe. She'd ask Percival Wellington tomorrow if there was a missing-persons bureau open yet in Barrie, and she'd get Pam to go into town with him and make inquiries. Food and other necessities were going to be a problem if the emergency lasted much longer. It was irritating to live in someone else's home and make so little contribution. She felt like an imposter, despite the billeting allowance Mrs. Wellington was getting from the authorities. And Andy—he bothered Percival with his "Why this?" and "How come you do that?" Over everything was the wretchedness of not having Jock with her, especially now when she needed him so badly.

She was about to move from the window when a car's headlights cut through the bare woodlot near the side road. The car turned in at the old cart track and its headlights suddenly went out. She strained to see it as it slowly approached the farmhouse. Why would someone douse their lights like that? And creep up to the house so quietly? Only if they didn't want to be seen or heard. The realization swept over her that someone intended to break in, and she clutched her throat to stifle the warning cry that arose. She tried very hard to see better. The car stopped and a door on one side opened. Two dark figures dropped to the ground, crouched on the icy gravel path, motionless, and then moved silently toward the house. Her heart thudded, and she had a suffocating feeling in her chest as the figures vanished around the side of the building. She looked into the room and back to the driveway, half convinced that she'd imagined it all. She'd been through so much lately, and the strain of the past three or four days, and worrying about . . .

Her hope was suddenly squelched when she heard the sound

of wood being carefully splintered. She regained her self-composure; the sight of two phantom figures had frightened her more than the noise made by two human housebreakers.

She calmly walked to the bedroom door, crossed the hall, and rapped on Percival's door. She heard his snoring, and tapped louder. His breathing rose and fell in long-sounding waves, up and down, in and out, with a period of silence at the crest and trough of each wave. She opened the door, crossed the room, and shook him. Instantly his eyes blinked open. "Chores time already?" he said in a sleepy voice.

"It's me—Alice MacGregor. Wake up. There're burglars downstairs!"

"Burglars!" She slapped a hand over his mouth.

"Shh—two men. They drove up—in a car. I think they're trying to break in the side door."

Percival threw aside the covers and jumped up, reaching for the shotgun he kept on a bracket over his bed. He loaded the gun and whispered to Alice to stay at the top of the landing, then crossed the room and climbed a ladder to the attic. Silently he tiptoed to the opposite side of the house, gently opened a small bow-shaped window, and stuck out his head. Thirty feet directly below two men were bending their weight on an iron bar they had jammed in the edge of the side door.

He pushed the gun through the window but the opening was too narrow to line up the target, so he pulled the trigger and popped his head forward at the same time. The gun roared and the shots peppered the ice-coated yard. A cry came from below. The iron bar clanged to the ground and two figures raced down the drive. As they disappeared Percival ran down the ladder and rushed into the room occupied by Mrs. MacGregor and Pamela.

"What's going on?" Pamela yelled, sitting up in a tangle of sheets, her eyes wide open.

"It's all right!" Her mother had followed Percival into the room. He strode to the window, yanked up the wide sash, and poked the gun out.

"I'll blast yer," he shouted, peering into the darkness. He saw the dim form of the car and heard the door slam.

"Jest for good measure," he yelled, and fired the second barrel. The lead pinged on the roof of the car, and shattered glass tinkled on the gravel. The engine roared, the back axle whining as the driver backed up the old cart track. The sound slumped, then headlights flashed, swiveled, and the car raced down the sideroad.

"That'll teach 'em!" Percival growled self-righteously.

"Call the police," Alice MacGregor said.

"Don't worry. They won't come back in no 'urry. Not now they know about old Betsy 'ere." He patted the gun as Pamela switched on the table lamp. "Everybody'd better get back to bed."

Both Andy and Mrs. Wellington slept through the racket, and before the old lady appeared at breakfast the next morning Percival told Andy about the intruders.

"Robbers!" Andy cried.

"Shh, shut up—Ma'll hear yer, young 'un!"

The attempted break-in made Alice MacGregor more uneasy, more anxious for an end to the emergency and a return to the city. Shadows had appeared under her eyes and her face was pinched. She helped to clear away the breakfast things and talked with Percival about taking Pamela into town to find out about a missing-persons bureau. Pamela was doing the dishes in the kitchen, listening to the EMO station on Mrs. Wellington's ancient radio.

"I'll be out in the back," Andy said. "Let me know when you're going to town with Mr. Wellington. I wanna come too."

Pamela turned up the volume on the radio so that she could hear it above the splashing water.

". . . householders are again reminded that only EMO officials wearing armbands or in uniform are authorized to enter homes for the purpose of making billeting arrangements with the owners. In several cases, unauthorized persons impersonating EMO or other officials have gained entry into houses. Armed robberies have been reported in some areas. The official government authority repeats its earlier message: do not allow persons you do not know entry into your house unless . . ."

"Mom, did you hear that? I bet those were holdup men last night. We'd better report it to the police when we go into town," Pamela called from the kitchen.

"I told Mr. Wellington, but he said not to bother," her mother replied. "Seems like they're used to that sort of thing in the country. Give me the city any time," she added, with feeling.

There had been at least half a dozen robberies in the Barrie area under pretense of being official calls. Further north, near Midland, gangs of young hoodlums from the city had gone around some of the reception areas molesting girls in the females-only centers before the provincial police and EMO officials had had time to set up command posts and take security measures. The gangs had cut the electric-power cables to one temporary hut and terrorized a group of women and children for more than an hour before one of the girls broke loose and ran for help. The culprits escaped, but a nervous soldier shot and seriously wounded one.

Crimes against the living were understandable under the

circumstances, but there were also outrages perpetrated against the dead. Ghouls preyed on the truckloads of bodies carted at night to the huge communal graves hacked out of the frozen ground by the earth-moving machines. They hid in cars parked out of sight in the trees and before the burial parties could organize their grim work they stole up to the trucks and tore gold and diamond rings off the stiff fingers of the corpses, wrenched billfolds and coins from pockets, and ripped off topcoats and jackets.

The Royal Canadian Mounted Police alerted the armed forces, and thereafter soldiers rode the death trucks to guard the bodies being taken for burial. Three body robbers creeping behind a truck met with a burst of fire from a soldier's weapon, and sprawled in a bloody heap in the snow. The officer commanding the patrol conferred for a few seconds with the senior EMO official: the three warm bodies were thrown into the grave with the bodies they had tried to rob.

The authorities managed to keep the news of these isolated outbreaks from the overcrowded refugee communities scattered throughout the countryside, but the evacuees grew more restless under the hardships of an irregular food supply, ineffectively organized medical help, and the overwhelming bereavements that hit some families. To add to the misery, a flu epidemic raged through the centers. The government responded by thinning out the population in the reception centers, sending people by special trains to private billets in Windsor, Ottawa, northern Ontario, Montreal, and as far away as Winnipeg, where they could be dispersed and the radiation sickness cases receive better medical treatment.

By the end of the first week of the evacuation grim rumors started to fly. A policeman at Aurora control headquarters overheard a scientist's remark about the feared change in direction of the radioactive plume from Fairfield and the risk of pollution to water supplies if it fell on the lake. He mentioned it to a buddy in the overcrowded eating quarters, and a helicopter pilot from Aurora, on a communications flight north, landed at an emergency heliport near Barrie and told another pilot about the latest worry at Aurora.

"The eggheads think it'll poison the drinking water," he said seriously. He was the most recent arrival from headquarters, and what he said implied official thinking. The rumor spread with every car and truck that left Barrie. Traffic to the outlying towns was light, since gas stations had run out of supplies, but there was still a steady flow of people between the larger places. When a whisper about a black market in drinking water rustled through the countryside the authorities decided it was time to act. A carefully worded announcement was made on the emergency radio network.

"This is an official government announcement of the gravest urgency . . ." Pamela reached out and turned the volume higher. ". . . reports that the drinking water is being affected by the radioactive discharge from the Fairfield Nuclear Power Station are entirely without foundation. The latest word from the emergency control headquarters at Aurora a few miles north of Toronto is that the discharge from the station is not—repeat, *not*—contaminating the source of water used for drinking purposes. Water for drinking purposes in the Barrie area and in other municipalities around Lake Simcoe comes directly from this lake. No contamination of any sort is reported. A constant check is being kept on the purity of all water supplies. Communities further north also have no need to worry."

Pamela instinctively took her hands out of the water in the sink, dried them, and looked at her fingernails.

"We're all right," Percival Wellington said confidently. "Our water supply comes from the lake, clean as a whistle.

We've got our own supply, from the 'lectric pump in the base-ment—near the laundry tubs."

"But what if the water in the lake's contaminated?" Pamela asked.

"But it ain't. You jest heard the man on the radio."

"Yes, I know. But supposing it is?"

"Then we'd all be poisoned, that's what," Percival re-plied, and shrugged his shoulders. He passed a horny hand through his thinning hair and sighed. Pamela let the water out of the sink, being careful when she pulled on the plug chain not to get her hands wet, and started to dry the dishes. The radio announcer had switched to other official reports and was giving the latest information on what was going on at Fair-field. "Top-ranking nuclear experts and engineers from four countries—the United States, Canada, Britain, and France—are now meeting at headquarters control to work out a scheme to end the radioactive discharge. A solution is very close at hand."

Alice MacGregor, helping Pamela put the cups and saucers away, snorted: "How close is very close?" She wondered about their bungalow near the power station, and had an image of the dust and grit from the plant creeping through the cracks in the storm windows and covering her hardwood floors with radioactive burns, or whatever radioactivity did.

"Shh, Mom! *Please!* They're coming to the family an-nouncements!" Pamela turned the volume still higher.

"Here is the latest official list of missing persons and persons seeking them . . ."

Pamela raised her finger to her lips and silently threaded the drying cloth through the rack behind the door.

"The list is in alphabetical order. Here are the *A*'s. Laura Adams, 144 Edward Boulevard, Toronto, is reported at Re-ception Center Number Eight at Orillia. Informs Mr. Arthur

Adams, husband, and children Frederick and Nancy. Mr. Norman L. Adams, 1266 Forest Avenue, Scarborough, Toronto, informs wife, Mrs. Jocelyn Mary Adams, he is with children Olga, Teddy and Barbara at the Staples Farm, Rural Route Number One, Lindsay, and has no news of either his wife or Betty Anne . . ."

Alice MacGregor sighed. This was the fourth time she'd listened to the announcements. Each time she'd seen the agony in Pamela's face as the end of the *A*'s came and went, and the announcer started on the *B*'s. She stared at the broken linoleum on the floor.

"That is the end of surnames beginning with the letter *A*," the voice said dispassionately, seemingly unconcerned with the tens of thousands of listeners who clung to every name, every initial, waiting breathlessly for him to mention a certain street and number.

"Here are the *B*'s. Mr. Kenneth R. Bates, of 36 Warren Road, Scarborough, Toronto, is reported at Reception Center Nine, Gravenhurst . . ." Pamela froze, sucked in her breath, hands crunched tightly together. ". . . with his mother; informs Miss Pamela MacGregor. Mrs. Ellen Bavola, of—"

"Catch her!" Alice MacGregor cried, as Pamela collapsed on the floor.

ELEVEN

The wind held steady for two days, and the sounding balloons General Waring had released to float over the city stayed almost stationary in the clear sky. As the sun warmed the city the weak air currents carried the balloons upward until they entered the high-altitude air streams, gathered speed, and were whisked away to the west, tracked by radar.

So far, so good. But how much longer the fine weather would hold worried the Department of Transport meteorologists. The meteorological branch at the Toronto International Airport had not reopened since the airport had been evacuated, and weather reports were being radioed directly to General Waring's headquarters at Aurora from all parts of the North American continent. The weather experts in the little room adjoining the main conference room where Deighton and his group were working deciphered the data and drew lines on blank weather maps. That the ballons drifted west when they rose into higher altitudes was a good sign: it meant that a high-pressure center in northern Ontario was fairly stable. But the thing they worried about was a low-pressure system in Kansas that was slowly moving east. If it gathered strength from a north-flowing stream of moist air coming up from the Gulf, it might push the fair weather away from Ontario and hurl blasts of snow-laden cold air from the Midwest into the region.

Rheinheimer's anxiety that the wind would suddenly veer to the northwest and blow the contamination over Lake Ontario, although possible, was unfounded, momentarily at least. After General Waring had assured him that the slightest change in the wind pattern would be spotted immediately, he thought the matter over and decided there was nothing more he could do to keep the danger uppermost in the minds of those at emergency control headquarters. But he took no chances. He telephoned Washington and instructed the Radiological and Biological Division of his department to maintain a continuous monitoring of the radioactivity level of the water being pumped through the intakes from the lake that supplied drinking water to Rochester and other cities on the south shore. He also instructed that samples of the air over Rochester and even Albany, less than a hundred miles from New York City, be checked hourly.

Since the second day of the evacuation, he and other United States experts, together with Deighton and the others, had settled into a razor-edge existence at control headquarters. News of the terrible deaths up north had trickled in, and the faces around the operations table were haggard from worry and lack of sleep. Deighton's group had been separated from the rest so that they could carry on with their plans to build a containment dome over the exposed fuel bundles at the station.

On the third day a group of volunteers had been air-lifted from Aurora in a helicopter and landed a half mile from the plant. Six men had been chosen to work in teams of two to more precisely assess the damage at the station. Deighton had calculated that each man could stay in the heavily contaminated area for six minutes before using up his three months' allowance of radiation absorption, but he had decided to cut this in half—to allow each man only three minutes within the station grounds. That would mean a total of eighteen minutes for the assessment survey by the six men: they would have to work fast.

They couldn't use the air-cooled suits MacGregor had worn because the air supply had been cut off at the station. They relied on the heavy coveralls, hard rubber boots, and respirators, and each man carried a dosimeter and geiger counter as well as his ordinary film badge.

The expedition went well, but brought back disturbing news. Number One reactor had overheated during the shutdown operation and the heavy-water pressure tubes had burst. The radioactive water had gushed out and flooded the chamber from which the bundles had been removed. Deighton's experts were faced with another problem: how to pump away the fiercely "hot" water that was now exposed to the atmosphere and the wind.

Johnson was speaking in the conference room. During the night he'd been on the telephone with AECB head office in Ottawa getting details on the similar heavy-water flood that had occurred in 1952 at the Atomic Energy of Canada research station at Chalk River, about 125 miles northwest of Ottawa.

"I know you lifted out the heart of the reactor then, but it weighed less than three tons. That's impossible to do at Fairfield," he said to Deighton, who sat in his shirt sleeves. It was uncomfortably fusty in the room; with so many people in the underground center the air-conditioning system was overloaded.

"If we're forced to seal up the reactor building after we pump out the heavy water it'll be a year before anyone can get in!" Johnson exclaimed, calculating the natural rate of radio-active decay. He rubbed his chin, rough with stubby growth. The strain was beginning to show—there were gray patches under his eyes and the muscles around his mouth were tight. Neither he nor the owners of the station, the Hydro-Electric Commission of Ontario, would tolerate the station closing down for a year. For no other reason than that his body was tired and his brain fatigued, Rita came pressing in on his thoughts.

She'd probably left town after all, but only after she'd been ordered. She never moved with the crowd, although she liked being part of the crowd. A self-determined loner with strongly entrenched ideas, based on the idea of Rita-first, Rita-second, and Rita-third. He distrusted career women. They were self-centered and grasping. Too masculine, too, although he could never level that charge at Rita. She was femininely sexy and provocative, and he couldn't deny she had a most attractive figure. In some ways he felt inadequate, especially when they were in public. Men looked at Rita and moved their eyes over her body—he could almost hear their thoughts.

Things might have worked out differently if she'd left Woman's Wondawear after they'd married. They might have had a kid or two; he'd have liked that. She used her looks as a defense. "Let's wait a year. You can't expect me to work if my figure . . . and you want me to help save for the house we plan, don't you darling?"

"We can't settle for temporary measures!" Deighton's voice, sharply irritated, dispelled his thoughts. "Johnson, how's the work on the dome coming? Have they got over the trouble with the lead shield?" he asked, referring to the huge dome now being hurriedly built at a nuclear engineering workshop in Montreal.

EPICENTER

"I checked first thing this morning, sir. It'll be ready for tests tomorrow."

The decision to build the dome over the fuel bundles had been made several days ago. The structure would be railed and trucked to Toronto in sections and assembled over the bundles and smashed shielding by teams of skilled workers operating in relays. It had been decided to solve the transportation problem by towing the heavy dome away, once the bundles and concrete were enclosed, by powerful tractors stationed several hundred yards distant. The tractors were being fitted with lead-lined cabs at the General Motors' factory in Oshawa, a few miles east of Toronto. Special equipment had been hastily installed to work the lead sheets, and a team of experts with advanced knowledge of heavy earth-moving equipment had been flown in from International Harvester's plant in Chicago. Both Johnson and Deighton were certain that the thing would work, and now they were bringing their resources to bear on the radioactive water leak.

Society in general had recovered from the first onslaught of the disaster. There was a breathing spell as men and equipment reeled and then recovered from the initial shock of the sudden dispersal. The rush of deaths had slowed, and the radiation sickness cases in the outlying medical centers had been surveyed and a victim count made.

In Parliament the Opposition was threatening to make a political issue out of the unpreparedness of the authorities and the general disorder and mix-up in government signals, although the Prime Minister had successfully thwarted the Opposition's attempts to call for a vote of confidence. He stood by his decision to declare a national emergency for the southern Ontario area. But his critics were hot on the trail: a public outcry in the antigovernment newspapers was stirring up trouble that was bound to break as soon as life returned to normal. Editorial opinion was strongly critical of the policy that allowed nuclear stations to be built near large urban centers. Although denying that anything was wrong with the policy, the government had stopped all work on two other nuclear power stations under construction—one near Montreal and another on the shore of Lake Huron.

An almost-tangible hiatus crept like a benediction through the underground rooms and little chambers and storerooms in the Aurora headquarters. It even touched flint-hard General Waring, who at that moment was standing in front of a map of southern Ontario showing Ferrisston, Rheinheimer, and top-ranking EMO officials where most of Toronto's population had settled. They sat around a table on which reports from the radio communications switchboard next door stood in untidy piles. Waring struck the map with a tapered pointer.

"The bulk of the evacuees are in the towns forming a rough crescent between forty and seventy miles out," he said. "From Peterborough over here, north to Midland, and west through Waterloo and Kitchener right down to Windsor on the United States border. Many people have, fortunately, doubled up with relatives and friends in the centers even further north and east, plus of course those who have opened up their summer cottages and are making do as best they can. At least they're clear of radiation and biological danger." He glanced at Rheinheimer and then stood back and stared at the map. He felt strangely uncertain. The recovery from the first shock of the accident, the knowledge that men were hammering, machining, riveting, and assembling equipment to stem the flow of radioactivity from Fairfield—these facts somehow failed to reassure him that everything was under control. The unknown factor of the wind direction when the weather pattern ultimately changed hung over everything, a worry he could not push to the back of his mind. He was tormented by the knowledge that he could do nothing to control the wind. He couldn't even take precautions. Nobody knew from which direction it would blow when it started up.

He turned from the map, but before he could sit down the soundproof door of the radio communications room burst open and an operator stuck his head out.

"Sir—please pick up your phone immediately. There's an urgent message."

Waring grabbed the instrument, and as he listened he paled. His big frame crumpled, and he grasped the back of the chair. Then his eyes flashed, he stiffened, and he dropped the telephone. But when he faced the room and spoke, his voice was under perfect control.

"Toronto is on fire!" he said deliberately, and calmly picked up a red telephone.

TWELVE

For the second time in two days Joe Griffiths sat in a truck racing toward Toronto. The vehicle that bounced uncomfortably along deserted suburban Yonge Street was in a hurtling caravan of fire-fighting vehicles. The water pumpers had taken a route from the outskirts. They had been driven there from the downtown fire stations the night of the big exodus, standard EMO practice for an emergency of such magnitude. Other fire equipment had also been driven clear of the city and parked in outlying schoolyards set up as temporary fire stations. When General Waring picked up the red telephone he set in motion a well-oiled machine in which Joe Griffiths and his comrades, under Captain Anders, were small but vital cogs.

The emergency fire crew members were dressed in protective suits and high rubber boots and wore respirators. Griffiths had trouble with the unfamiliar fireman's helmet. He preferred the more conventional hardhat or even the old British Army steel helmet that he had worn during the war. He pulled the thing over his head and cursed as the strap tangled with the heavy rubber bands of the respirator, which cut into his face.

EPICENTER

The truck slowed and stopped. Anders poked his head through the little window. "Everybody check dosimeters," he ordered. The heads of the other members of the team bent as they glanced at the instruments clipped to their suits. "Check respirators secure," Anders called. "We're gonna act as reserves for the regular fire service. We'll wait here for further instructions." He turned and listened to the chatter on the radio, mentally reviewing the principles of fire fighting he'd learned at the EMO training course.

The fire had been spotted by a reconnaissance plane that had been flying in a check pattern over the city since dawn. The pilot had reported a vertical column of black smoke rising somewhere in the downtown core where the old narrow houses were crowded. He estimated that the smoke rose a hundred feet before it petered out in a smudge and dispersed. He continued his zigzag pattern over the city, and an Otter aircraft, which was able to fly at slow speed, was dispatched to take a closer look. The plane was equipped with radiation-monitoring equipment to warn the pilot of contamination danger. He flew over the column at six thousand feet—the lowest he dared go with the needle on the radiation gauge edging up to the red mark—and radioed that the smoke was coming from a chimney. On his third banked turn around he reported a red glow from the top of the chimney. The message was flashed to General Waring and the EMO firefighting division.

Regular firemen had been surprised that they had not been called out before; it seemed impossible for two million people to leave a city in winter without hundreds leaving an electric or gas stove on. Scores of times every winter the fire department was called out to tend to overheated furnaces and blazes caused by old-fashioned stoves, and it had been a miracle that a serious fire hadn't broken out so far. There were millions of ways a fire smoldering for the past week might suddenly ignite, but the clear, windless days and nights had helped to reduce the risk. Gusty weather would have chilled empty houses and caused thermostats to turn on. As it was, thousands of houses had used up their oil supplies, and automatic furnaces were silent in frigid basements. Water systems froze, and icy patterns were oozing from burst plumbing fixtures.

When General Waring received the signal that smoke had been spotted he knew what could happen, and he had a deep suspicion that the contamination level at the source of the smoke was too high to allow fire fighters to get near it. He was a realist. His fears and subsequent reaction were perfectly normal under the circumstances.

Griffiths made a hopeless movement with his eyes. The last thing he wanted to become involved in was a fire-fighting operation—he'd done enough of that during the air raids. He'd preferred doing what he knew to be more dangerous work with the bomb-disposal and demolition squad he'd been transferred to. Fire was too unpredictable, but if a bomb exploded while he was defusing it, he'd never know anything about it.

"If it's got your number on it, it's got your number on it, if you know what I mean," he'd told his buddy, who'd nodded sagely.

He patiently sat in the covered truck as units of the Toronto Fire Department roared past, their sirens strangely silent as they raced down the deserted streets and braked at the checkpoints radio control had directed them to. For the first time in his thirty years' experience, the chief fire marshal, controlling operations from the Aurora base, was working under conditions every fireman secretly prayed for—no traffic to fight and no people to save. But he too was a realist, enough to know that over everything hung the threat of radioactivity that would stop his men from getting near the actual fire.

EPICENTER

He kept half his fire-fighting force as reserves in the outskirts, committed another quarter at standby in the uptown area, and arranged the rest in a circle around the area in which the house with the burning chimney was located.

The fire captain in the downtown area radioed that the contamination was too high to let his men approach closer than twelve blocks to the now-flaring chimney. A quick reference to the monitoring reports from the planes told fire control that no suit designed could protect a man at the level of radioactivity near the outbreak. The outlook was frightening: the fire had a free run in a densely packed district.

Minutes after the Otter pilot's message the roof of the tenement house caught fire, and a wide column of black smoke billowed skyward. On the radio Griffiths heard the fire captain nearest the blaze do something against which every instructor warned his students: get angry with a fire. His anger was born of sheer frustration, his utter helplessness at his inability to fight the blaze. In normal conditions, ten minutes with a standard pumper and he'd be ready to reach for a blank fire-report form.

The roofs on each side of the blazing house caught fire, and the flames quickly ran down the walls of the wooden frame structures. Old paint blistered under the searing heat and popped sparks across a narrow lane toward houses in the adjoining block. The aircraft reported several houses on fire and long flames clearly visible.

"Try the count now!" Griffiths heard the urgency in the demand from fire control. The radio fell silent while the fire captain nearest the scene detailed his squad to test. Overlying the crackle from the speaker Griffiths imagined he could hear a faint roaring sound.

"Off the top limit two hundred yards from the truck!" the captain barked. Everything went quiet again, and Griffiths strained to hear the discussion in the background, gruff voices that spoke fast.

"Keep a constant check and report any change either way!" the order came through. "Stand by in your present position!"

The brick houses across the street were next to ignite. The flames leapt from the pile of burning debris—all that remained of the wooden houses—and fingered the dry wood doors and window frames. Like an uninvited stranger seeking admittance, the fingertips touched the panels, grew bolder, grasped the door. Fiery fingers turned to muscular fists that imperiously hammered for entry, and suddenly a torrid shoulder demanded entrance and blasted open the doors with an incandescent blow of searing flame and sparks. The flames swept through the blackened entranceways and burst into the front rooms, consuming everything—scratched dining tables, stuffed chairs, ragged carpets, buffets, worn drapes, walls, floorboards—and rushed with a great roar up the stairs, eating them alive. The fire wall exploded through the roofs, shooting up a shower of sparks, charred roof timbers, and chunks of flaming asphalt tile.

The circling planes, keeping above six thousand feet, flashed a message to fire control. Waring now stared at the large-scale map of downtown Toronto that had replaced the one of southern Ontario on the wall. The chief fire control officer peered at the street names, and with a crayon scribbled in radiation figures. The general thought of water-bombing the fire with forestry fire-control planes, but he quickly dismissed the idea; the planes would have to drop their water loads from two hundred feet, too low for pilot safety.

White-hot ashes started to fall in the streets near the burning houses, and a gentle breeze sprang up as the hot smoke rose higher over the city and sucked in cooler air from the outer perimeter. Igneous bits of cinder floated farther from the center of the roaring fire, and thirty minutes after the first message to General Waring three blocks of decrepit houses and shops were blazing. The fire advanced in little leaps and rushes, hopscotched over streets, reached across the wider chasms, and attacked the three-story retail stores and grubby commercial offices on the boundary of the downtown business district.

The red tongues licked the wooden railings of municipal parking lots. They devoured the pine streetlight poles, which crashed to the ground, smashing the iron lamp brackets bolted to the tops. The overhead cables fell in festoons, the insulation material flaring angrily like pyrotechnic snakes at a monster fireworks display. Rivulets of sizzling tar dripped from the storefronts on Queen Street as the pitch on the roofs melted, forming hot icicles that clung momentarily to the overhang of the store windows before falling in burning torrents to the sidewalks. Store windows exploded in showers of sparkling powder, melting and coagulating into translucent pools that reflected red-and-yellow flames. The gutters ran with liquid fire as the molten glass swept up the burning tar and rushed with quicksilver haste to the nearest drain.

The fire crept inexorably onward and outward, and from the air the circle of flame blossomed, a crimson flower unfolding under a strong sun. The petal tips touched the modern high-rise apartment blocks on the fringe of the old part of the city, the white-faced buildings blackening under the hungry flames. Windows burst and glowed as tongues of fire flashed over sills and gulped curtains and furniture. The solid structures withstood the onslaught momentarily, but the terrific heat turned each floor into a fiery crucible. The flames flew upward from story to story, crumbling walls and floors, drawn by some massive invisible suction. They erupted with volcanic force and blew the roofs skyward, blasting up pillars of fire in a furious turmoil of hot black smoke.

The billows met a warm layer of air at four thousand feet and flattened out. The smoke spread laterally, and the watchers in the sky reported that a veil of smoke now partly obscured the fire.

Griffiths stared upward, watching the edges of the cloud turn black. The creases between his nose and mouth deepened, and he took a huge mouthful of air through his respirator, expelling it in a gust that fogged his goggles.

"Blasted fire!"

Anders glanced at Griffiths and then at the darkening sky. Through the open window he could feel a wind stir as the cooler air quickened from the surrounding area.

Griffiths peered through the little sliding window communicating with the cab. Four fire trucks were drawn up in the middle of the street about two blocks away, and above them the first flames began to show near the distant buildings. He could sense the helplessness of the regular force firemen as they watched the fire approach, opening and closing their fists in tight balls of frustration. The fire in the distance burst into a white glow, silhouetting the trucks in stark outline. The pavement had crumbled at the heart of the fire, the flames grounding into a subterranean natural-gas pipeline. The welded seams buckled and blew apart under the tremendous heat, and flames hungrily engulfed the inexhaustible fuel in the exposed gas main. A searing heat wave rushed outward and scorched the red paint on the trucks. They backed up the street.

"Cut off the gas at the control valves nearest the fire!" General Waring barked when the radio crackled. "Why the hell wasn't that done before?"

EPICENTER

An EMO official ran to the map room and rushed back with a rolled chart under his arm. A man circled the control valves for the gas lines on the map, and the fire marshal radioed instructions to crews to close the valves. Some were in the area where the radioactivity was too strong to approach, and valves farther afield had to be located to cut off the gas feeding the huge sea of fire that roared toward the soaring skyscrapers and tall empty hotels.

The sounding balloons Waring had released outside the built-up area suddenly picked up speed and rode the air currents toward the flames. They raced like madmen to the swirling core, abruptly curved before reaching the fire, and flew upward crazily on the fast-rising hot air. The general ordered radiation measurements to be taken in the suburbs and farther afield, fearing that the contaminated air drawn into the maelstrom would move outward and drop on the countryside miles from the city.

Waring had one trump card to play. Now was the moment to use it. Griffiths heard the radio come to life. Anders bent to listen.

"We're gonna dynamite the buildings round the fire—make a firebreak!" he shouted. "We've got to pick up supplies at Depot Number Four. Okay, Bill, let's go!" he ordered. The engine roared. The driver swung the vehicle around and accelerated up the street. Griffiths was relieved he didn't have to go near the fire.

A long line of EMO trucks was drawn up outside the depot when they arrived, and it took some minutes for boxes of dynamite to be loaded and detonators gingerly laid on the felt-covered rack in the back of the truck. Anders received instructions by radio, and the truck sped toward the flames that flared up over the buildings in the near distance, stopping in a street in a business section about half a mile from the fire.

EPICENTER

Anders checked the monitoring instruments: the needle was at the top of the safety mark but still below the danger line.

"Everybody out! Joe, supervise the detonator handling. You others bring the dyno!" he shouted. His team was to lay the charges in the buildings that lined a street near fashionable Bloor Street, east of Yonge Street. On his flank another demolition crew would line their sector with charges; farther east, in a wide curving line, other dynamiters were hurrying into position.

Waring's idea was to kill the fire by destroying the material that fed it—buildings. His plan was to completely surround the hundred acres of fire with gaps wide enough to stop the flames from jumping across. It was a ruthless move, but if he hesitated now the city would be completely destroyed.

The demolition teams spread out quickly. The monitoring instruments in the eastern sectors reported the radiation level was too high to allow the men in. Waring gasped when he heard the news, and made a subdued sound in his throat. "Forget the east! Demolition squads stand by in case the level drops," he growled. "Carry on with the other sectors."

Griffiths strode to the row of twelve high buildings across the street, refurbished old houses that had been acquired by benevolent societies, trade associations, and insurance agencies.

"Start here!" Anders shouted, his voice muffled by the respirator. He nodded at the first house and went next door with his men. Griffiths directed two men with axes to batter down the front door. He went along the hall, found the basement door, and clambered down the stairs, hugging the cold metal detonators to his chest. Expert fingers quickly laid the charges among a nest he made of old ledgers and tattered index files.

"Add that up," he muttered. Anders appeared at the top of the steps.

EPICENTER

"How you doing down there, Joe?" he yelled.

"Ready to wire up!" Griffiths uncoiled the detonator cable drum and paid out the wires. He snaked them along the hallway and into the street. The same work was going on in the other houses, and the wires in the street were rapidly connected to a detonating cable leading back to the truck, parked some distance away. Griffiths checked that everybody was back in the truck before he hooked up the detonation switch.

"All ready," he reported to Anders.

Anders sucked in air through his respirator and gave a nod. Griffiths rammed the switch lever down with an experienced movement and looked out the little observation window. For a tiny moment nothing happened. Then the buildings erupted in a flash of flame and dense clouds of dust. He could see the rooftops shudder and blow upward, the walls shake and crumble. When the dust settled, all that was left of the block was a pile of debris with bricks and splintered wood strewn over the street. The flames in the distance seemed ominously closer across the rubble.

"Next block!" Anders ordered.

The driver cautiously moved forward, skirting the smoking debris. The heavy tires plink-plonked over smashed brickwork. A massive splintered roof beam blocked the way. Anders looked at the radiation monitor and nodded to two men through the window. They climbed down and heaved the timber out of the truck's path.

There was a row of about twenty retail shops in the next block—a grocery, a drugstore with post office, haberdashery, and variety stores. In the center was a high building with a carwash on the ground floor and two stories of bowling alleys above. Anders cast his eye along the street, expertly sizing up the amount of explosives needed and where he should position the truck for safety. Again Griffiths handled the detonators.

EPICENTER

The axes made short work of the store windows. It took six men to lay and connect the charges to the big bowling-alley building that stretched back to the street behind. They retired to the truck, now parked on a side street. Anders figured the blast would cut across the main street and ricochet off the high buildings opposite the doomed structures.

Griffiths wired the charges through a selection switch to make sure the nearest building would blow first, the others following as the high explosives ripped along the street. He pressed the switch. The blasts shook the truck, high pressure waves pounding on the reinforced metal roof as they huddled inside. Griffiths took his fingers out of his ears momentarily to listen to the bangs farthest away. He nodded when he heard the duller thumps as the extra charges he'd laid in the basement of the carwash exploded.

The cacophony subsided, and they heard the roar of the explosives of the other wrecking crews in the neighborhood. When they had blown their fifth blast, with Anders checking radiation levels before he ordered each move forward, they had teamed up with two other demolition squads. The three lines of firebreaks had merged, and a gash a hundred yards wide was shaping around the center of the downtown core. Twenty-story hotels had been blown apart in the midtown district, and block-long department stores, a big Woolworth's, and massive high-rise apartment structures toppled in a series of explosions as the crews systematically leveled everything outlined in red crayon on their maps.

The air was dusty and acrid. Tiny bits of debris fell in a light rain that covered the lenses of the men's goggles. Beyond the cleared area they could hear the crackle of flames. Anders conferred with the fire captains. They checked the monitoring gauges and shook their heads. It was too dangerous to approach beyond the firebreak.

Waring jammed the receiver closer to his ear and then brightened. "That'll halt it!" he said grimly. "Don't worry about the eastern sector." He rubbed the back of his neck, trying to unlock the tight cords. A fire captain jotted a red line on the map, completing the outline of the firebreak that almost encompassed the fire. The general studied the map intently as he waited for the first signal that the flames had reached the firebreak and had started to burn out. He ordered the fire marshal at control to instruct all demolition squads and fire-fighting crews to retire to stand-by distance.

"Everybody in the truck," Anders ordered when he received the message. The other crews jumped aboard their vehicles. Anders' truck drove around the wrecked remains of the midtown Northbury Hotel. Griffiths, peering from the small wire-gridded window, was amazed to see a battered legless bed as they went past, the blankets and sheets still neatly tucked in, just as the chambermaid had left them.

He looked back at the fire that swept across his narrowing vision as the truck retired. A widening black pall hung over the city, obscuring the sun. He looked at his watch: it was nearly five o'clock. He'd been on the go for ten hours.

They stopped. Anders stuck his head close to the window. "We'll wait here on stand-by. If anybody's feeling hungry there's a cake shop across the road and the windows are loaded with goodies. I won't look if somebody accidentally breaks in."

Everyone laughed. "Let's go!" a man said. Anders turned to speak to the driver. He heard the crash of tinkling glass, and a minute later Griffiths poked his hand through the sliding window and offered him a bun. Anders took it, half jokingly held it up to the radiation monitor, and pressed his teeth into the stale dough.

THIRTEEN

"Trona's on fire!" someone yelled in the schoolhouse. "I just heard it on the radio!"

Rita felt a cold shock of terror vibrate through her body. She fought to bring her feelings under control, and turned to Rosie Long. The two women were sitting at one of the trestle tables, drinking coffee they had drawn from a large urn.

"It's burning and they can't get the fire out!" the newsmonger, a boy about seventeen, shouted.

"Hey—stow that, will yer!" a rugged EMO man cried. "What're yer tryin' to do? Panic all these women 'ere?"

The youth stared at him. "It's true, I tell you. Listen for yourself!" He took the transistor radio he hugged to his ear and offered it to the man.

"I already knows about it. It came over the special EMO radio. It does no good to broadcast it around, 'specially at a time like this."

"Aw—baloney!" the youth said disgustedly, and shuffled out of the door, the radio at his ear.

Rosie Long peered over the others, trying to see Shirley.

EPICENTER

The girl was sitting at the back of a knot of children watching a portable television set one of the evacuees had brought.

Rita recovered. "She's okay, Rosie. I can see her. I wonder if it's true? About the fire, I mean."

"It's not a wonder. What with everybody out of the city and all them fires left burning," Rosie replied logically. "I wish I knew what the truth of it all is."

Rita had expected Rosie to be alarmed, and she wondered at how placidly she'd reacted. That's often the case with working-class people, she philosophized, now that she was calmer. They haven't got any imagination and can't see beyond the immediate present. Then she thought about her apartment, and her belongings, the china pieces, her traditional furniture, the figurines of genuine alabaster. What if they were destroyed in the fire? Her place was miles from downtown, but suppose the fire spread? And Women's Wondawear. That could go too. That'd put paid to her job. But everybody in the trade knew who she was. She wouldn't have any trouble getting another managerial job.

Rosie surprised her again. "How come they can't get the fire out—if what that kid said is true?"

"It's 'cos of the radiation. Won't let the firemen get near it," an elderly man sitting near her replied. He'd been quietly smoking his pipe, listening to the conversation.

"Oh," Rita said, "I see." She smoothed a strand of hair back. "You think it's true, then?" she asked the thin-faced man.

He nodded confidentially and bent close. "I heard about it last night," he said in a low voice. "My son's in the EMO and works close to here. Don't tell anybody I told you."

"How bad is it?" Rita asked.

The man glanced over his shoulder and leaned closer. "He

says all of Yonge Street's gone, from the lake up to St. Clair Avenue!"

Rita took a deep breath. It was the downtown district then, not the suburbs. Her place would be well out of it. She turned to Rosie to ask her where her house was, just as Shirley approached.

"Don't say nothin' about the fire," Rosie whispered hastily.

"Hi," Rita said. "Good movie on TV?"

The girl shook her head. She was bored. She'd grown accustomed to the crude living conditions but had kept apart from the few girls of her own age in the schoolhouse. She smiled faintly, looking at Rita's face, which was lit up with a friendly greeting. Mrs. Johnson wasn't like most of the others, thought Shirley. They stared at her mouth, and then watched her fingers, waiting for her to signal in deaf-mute signs. She wondered if Mrs. Johnson had children of her own, and how old they were.

The assembly hall was gloomy as the late-afternoon sun dropped below the horizon. Someone switched on the lights.

"I didn't think it was so late," Rosie said, rising. "I'd better go and see if they need help in the kitchen."

Neither woman spoke as the Mustang rolled toward the village intersection. Rita turned the car into a street that would take them to the hill on the Orillia road. Several cars overtook them as others out to see the distant sky over Toronto drove to the lookout spot. It was past eleven, and Rosie had checked that Shirley had fallen asleep before accepting Rita's offer to watch the red glare everybody said could be seen on the horizon.

"Mind yer back before midnight!" the EMO man at the schoolhouse door had warned.

"It'll be too far away to see anything," Rosie said dully,

breaking into Rita's thoughts. Rita had been thinking about her eventual return to the city, to her new place near the top of the high-rise. Everything would be quiet. She hated silent surroundings. They reminded her of cemeteries and museums and—death. Life is movement: the dead don't move. She shuddered, and consciously changed the trend of her thoughts. There'd be a lot to do when she returned to Women's Wondawear. That new stock she'd ordered in Montreal would have arrived, at least the first shipment. It probably had started to come in the day before the sirens had gone off. The rest would be delivered soon, when the emergency was over, unless the trains were delayed. They'd better deliver the stuff on time. The spring fashions had to be in the stores by early March, and she'd need time to evaluate the sales reports from the district managers. Everything had to be on schedule or her buying program and follow-through would fall apart.

"There's the reflection!" she exclaimed. They had reached the top of a long sloping country road where cars were parked on the soft shoulders. People stood in straggly lines on the humped frozen banks left by the snow plows. Rita braked, looking for a place to park. A horn sounded behind.

"Shut up!" she snapped, undecided whether to park or not.

"There's a place," Rosie said, pointing ahead. "On the other side of the road."

They left the car and walked back to where the others were looking across the dark countryside toward the city. A long, narrow streak of red glared angrily along the distant horizon, occasionally breaking into isolated flares that glowed brightly and subsided.

"Isn't it awful, Rita!" Rosie exclaimed. "How'll they put it out?"

"I don't know. But they'll do it. They've got to!"

EPICENTER

"It's dying down," Johnson exclaimed, stamping his feet on the snow. He was on top of the underground bunker at Aurora watching the sky over the burning city.

"There goes a big one!" Townsend cried. "Over to the east!" A great flash burst high into the air, flickered momentarily, and subsided in glimmering cascades of orange. A column of dense black smoke curled upward, clear cut against the strong light on the horizon.

"An oil-storage tank," someone muttered knowingly. "Saw 'em blow like that during the war." Johnson turned to see who had spoken, but the man said nothing more.

"We'd better get back," Deighton said sharply.

"The general'll think we're playing hooky," Johnson said to Townsend, who laughed self-consciously in the darkness.

The general had viewed the sight himself half an hour earlier, after receiving further reports from the fire fighters who waited in tight little groups at the street corners in the midtown districts. They'd expected the fire to rush up to the firebreaks, but the waves of flame were creeping outward at their own steady pace, slowing as they consumed large commercial buildings. But the firebreaks worked. The fire's intensity waned as it spread thinner in the outlying districts. The area east of Yonge Street, from the lakeshore through the central business and retail neighborhood to Bloor Street, was devastated, more than eight square miles of blackened twisted ruins. In the east the fire died by attrition as it approached open parkland at the north-running Don Valley Expressway. It sputtered at the snowline, rallied, then gave up trying to cross the wide ravine that divided the east of the city from the central region.

Deighton and his little group went back to their underground room. The chief fire marshal next door breathed easier, and General Waring sat in front of the map and sighed. Although he'd been on almost continuous duty for nearly two weeks and was tired, he looked as if he'd just come on to a parade ground for regimental inspection. It was past midnight, but his face was freshly shaven, his uniform immaculately pressed. He heard the scientists and engineers shuffling into the other room and decided to join them. When he entered he took a seat at the back and indicated with a subtle gesture of his head that he wanted Deighton to ignore him.

Deighton quickly summarized the progress for stopping the Fairfield leak. The first sections of the lead-lined dome had started to arrive at Oshawa. The dome would measure fifty feet across when fully assembled, and the massive sections were being loaded on railway flatcars at Montreal for their journey west. At Oshawa they would be transshipped to long tractor trailers and driven along Highway 401 to a coordinating point near Fairfield.

The machinery for the cutting blades had been assembled and tested at the General Motors plant, and the heavy-equipment experts had made preliminary studies for pulling the dome away when it had picked up its radioactive load.

But the other major problem remained: how to pump away the tons of radioactive heavy water that had gushed from the smashed pressure tubes of Number One reactor.

"Pumping is the least worry. We've got pipefitters and welders ready to lay a pipe from the chamber where the water lies to—to where?" Deighton asked. "We can't dump it in the lake, and there's nothing but houses around Fairfield; it's not as if we had sandy soil or a gravel pit nearby." He looked forlornly at the faces around the table.

"There's a gravel pit about half a mile away," Johnson said. "About here." He pointed to the map spread on the table. "It's this side of the highway, where the open country begins."

EPICENTER

Deighton perked up. He twirled the ends of his moustache furiously with his fingertips.

"Have you seen it?" he asked.

"Yes, I was down there for a stroll once," Johnson said in a flat tone, thinking of a fine summer day shortly after he'd married Rita. He'd shown her over the power station and afterward had driven around the district, exploring the neighborhood where they'd decided to settle. The gravel pit hadn't been worked for years, and the sides were overgrown with ragged grass and bushes. There was the hum of wild bees in the air as the insects hovered over the blue flowers that had sent roots into the sandy soil.

"Private property, no doubt," someone interjected.

"But it's not used now—all worked out," Johnson replied. "We don't have to worry about that, anyway, I'm sure."

"No, no," Deighton said. "We could commandeer land now."

"I can arrange the pumps and pipes," Johnson said enthusiastically, despite his fatigue. "It shouldn't take long, seeing that the distance is so short. I've worked out the amount of heavy water that must have leaked: about five thousand gallons."

"In that case, you could pump the lot through in less than half an hour," Deighton said, his face shining now. They were getting somewhere at last. Now that they were discussing pumping rates and hard metal fittings he felt much better. He glanced at General Waring listening at the back, and staring at the floor.

"Latest met reports show there's nothing serious heading this way. The calm air is likely to stay over the city for several more days," Deighton continued briskly. "We should have ideal working conditions."

Waring lifted his head and gave a little cough. "I just

wanted to add that the fire is burning itself out, as you probably saw for yourselves. The chief fire-control officer confirmed this a few minutes ago. Everything points to 'go.' "

"Very good, sir. What are the latest reports on radiation levels?"

"That picture looks good, too. We worried about the air moving upward and outward due to the fire, but we needn't have—the damned fire helped. The stagnant contaminated air over the city's been sucked in by the firewind and has now risen to a high altitude. It's spreading out over a wide area—over the countryside, in fact. The fire's helped disperse it."

"But we'll get fallout later," Rheinheimer said, a worried look on his wide face.

Waring looked at him tolerantly. A thick muscle worked under his chin. "My experts say it's nothing to worry about. The dispersal pattern is so wide and thin the fallout will be negligible. I've alerted the monitoring stations to check for any significant rise. Your stations on the other side will undoubtedly be doing the same." He knew about Rheinheimer's quiet instructions to monitor the air over New York State.

Rheinheimer seemed satisfied. He sat back and consulted some scientific journals he had taken from his briefcase, flipping the pages. It was clear that Waring had said all he intended to say.

"This is the schedule I've drawn up," Johnson said, pushing a sheaf of papers under Deighton's droopy mustache. "Perhaps we can discuss it now. We should soon be getting word that the dome's ready to take to Fairfield."

The call came from the factory at midday. A trial assembly had proved that the sections of the dome could be bolted together without any trouble. Johnson volunteered to establish a mobile base as near Fairfield as possible, directing operations by radio from close range.

"It'll be dangerous—the radiation levels, I mean," Deighton said, looking at him sharply.

"It's my station, sir," Johnson replied evenly.

He departed by helicopter at two o'clock. A monitoring patrol that had penetrated to within half a mile of the station reported radiation levels had diminished substantially since the fire. The helicopter settled north of Highway 401, where another monitoring team had set up a base with two instrument trucks and a mobile radio station. When Johnson landed he contacted Deighton to tell him where he was, and asked him to telephone Oshawa to get the dome sections moving.

He took off again in the helicopter, instructing the pilot to hover at a safe distance from the station so that he could see the gravel pit. His eye swept the ground below. Housing developments lay in prosaic patterns—nondescript bungalows, flat factory roofs, parking lots, winding deserted streets, with two or three cars nosed together here and there, the result of a pileup.

Over the dashboard he spotted the domes of the power station, lit with the glow from the afternoon sun like shafts of light on the turrets of a sultan's palace. Beyond lay the glittering blue waters of Lake Ontario, and farther out he could see the hazy United States shoreline forty miles away.

"There it is!" the pilot shouted, pointing. Johnson followed his finger. The shadow cast by the sun made the gravel pit appear as if a giant shovel had taken a huge scoop out of the earth and thrown in bucketloads of snow.

"Quite a way from the station," Johnson yelled. "We could lay pipes down that street." He indicated a dead-end street that ran to the edge of the pit. "Then along that road. Can you go left?" he shouted to the pilot.

"Sure. How far?"

"Just a bit. I want to trace a path to the station."

EPICENTER

"I'll slew her around," the pilot shouted, and the helicopter turned.

Johnson's keen eye followed the road to an intersection a few hundred yards away, where it picked up a suburban main road that led into the main entrance of the station.

"How far'd you say it is from the gravel pit to that intersection there?"

"What's that?"

Johnson shouted louder, bending toward the other. The pilot screwed up his mouth and furrowed his forehead.

"About quarter mile, maybe less," he decided.

"And from the intersection to—"

"Louder!"

"From the intersection to that wide road there!"

The pilot peered down. He twisted his mouth again. "Quarter mile!"

"Just over half a mile altogether, then?" Johnson yelled in the pilot's ear.

"Yep—not far off. Wanna gander this way?" The pilot swung the helicopter through another ninety-degree turn. Johnson gasped. He now had a clear view of the distant devastation. He pointed, and the pilot's eyes grew wide. Block after block of gridded streets lay in blackened ruins. The city had shrunk in size and height. Ashes and debris covered what had been roads, and scattered dark plinths stood isolated from the rest of the hollow buildings, remnants of burned-out apartments, office buildings, and hotels. Farther west the sun threw into dark relief the concrete buildings on the other side of the firebreaks, a line of demarcation between the living and the dead.

Johnson shouted: "Take years to clean up!"

He indicated to the pilot to turn away. "Hover while I make a sketch," he ordered. He took a pad of notepaper from his pocket and roughed in the outline of roads leading from the gravel pit to the station.

"Let's get back to base," he shouted. The rotor beat changed and the machine turned, losing height as the pilot searched the ground for the two trucks. He changed course and reduced speed. In a few minutes they landed next to the trucks.

Johnson checked the route for the pipeline on a map in the back of one of the trucks, and then radioed Deighton.

"Good. I'll organize the pipefitters," Deighton said. "Go over the route again." Johnson called out the street names on the map and Deighton drew a heavy line on the map he and General Waring had spread before them. The pipefitters, skilled men who had worked on the trans-Canadian natural-gas pipeline that swept from the gas fields of western Canada thousands of miles east to Ontario, had been mustered and now were standing by in the north end of the city. EMO officers briefed them on radiation dangers, and taught them how to read dosimeters and use the film badges. Deighton instructed them to work from the gravel pit toward the station; each four-man team, dressed in coverall suits and respirators, was to work under direct supervision of an experienced nuclear technician. Witzensky and his rescue team had been airlifted from Fairfield and would be responsible for guiding the pipemen into the station, under strict time limitations. Deighton stipulated that each man could spend only three minutes within the station environment, half the time they could theoretically stay without danger. He was taking no chances.

Floodlights were rushed into the gravel pit after a monitoring team had declared the area safe. At dusk Johnson drove to the pit by a circuitous route and stood in the road he'd spotted from the helicopter.

"The outlet pipe'll have to be buried at least thirty feet down," he explained to the head pipeman. "It's a soft pit so it'll drain well. Far enough from the lakeshore not to seep underground toward the water."

The pipemen erected a rig to drill through the pit. The snow and overburden were swept away by a bulldozer. Uneasy memories flooded back when Johnson heard the roaring machine. A thick pipe was driven into the pit and another pipe slanted toward the street. Long trucks drove up with sections of pipe, and welders expertly linked them. By midnight he reported to Aurora that the pipes had reached the intersection, and by three o'clock in the morning the welders were in sight of the main gates of Fairfield.

The bulky lead-lined dome sections were swung aboard eight low-loader trucks in Oshawa, and the journey to Fairfield began. By dawn the sections had almost reached Johnson's highway headquarters, and the trucks were parked down the middle of Highway 401. Two truckloads of assemblymen in protective suits had arrived earlier.

"The sections look fine," Johnson reported on the radio. "I'm sending a team in to inspect the reactor damage soon. Then we'll know where to locate the other end of the pipe— and how." He ran back to the convoy, and went from truck to truck, inspecting the steel-and-lead structures, each like a segment of peel stripped from some giant half-grapefruit.

"How's the pipelaying?" he asked the head pipeman, who'd come from the pipelaying site.

"Finished! Right up to the station gates almost. We were waiting for you to come to the official opening."

Johnson laughed. "Let's skip the ribbon-cutting ceremony. It's cold out here!"

He called together Witzensky's team, the dome erectors,

and pipemen. He lectured them on radiation dangers as they ate a cold breakfast washed down with hot coffee, flown in from Aurora by helicopter with other supplies.

"Nobody's permitted to remain inside the actual station grounds more than three minutes. Three minutes! There'll be pockets of higher radioactivity in some places, so check your dosimeters constantly. As the monitoring teams find hot spots, they'll stick up red warning flags. Any questions?"

There were none. Every man understood the danger and knew what he had to do. The sun shone from an almost cloudless sky. The trucks on the highway snorted into life. The final lap of the journey had begun.

Johnson jumped into his camp truck and reported the movement to Deighton.

"I've instructed Witzensky and the monitoring team to signal any change in radioactivity levels," he said.

"Have you checked again on how long it'll take to get the dome up, and if you've got enough men? The factory says only forty minutes are needed, according to their assembly tests," Deighton questioned anxiously.

"I've allowed sixty minutes. There're enough assemblers to do it in relays with their three-minute allowances, and there's the back-up team, just in case."

The workers had to make every second count. In five minutes the first reports started to come back from the monitoring team. The levels were lower than Johnson had estimated. A half hour later he was able to tell Deighton: "They've got six of the eight sections of the dome up. And we don't need that pipe after all! The heavy water's seeped away!"

FOURTEEN

Joe Griffiths peered at Anders through the transparent visor of the protective suit. The needle on the monitoring gauge of the counter registered zero. Satisfied that it was safe to go ahead, Anders spoke into the radio microphone mounted under the visor. The two men then walked across the wide street and stood on the broad deserted sidewalk outside the Regal Hall Hotel.

The helicopter that had deposited them in the middle of the street like visitors from another planet roared upward, hovered momentarily, then swung away across Lake Ontario. Griffiths glanced up as Anders tapped his shoulder and pointed to something on the sidewalk.

A thin black cat arched its body against the brass-framed revolving door of the hotel entrance. Its friendly eyes sparkled with pleasure at the sight of the two humans.

"Poor old puss!" Griffiths said loudly. "A waif from the storm!" He picked it up and cuddled it in the nook of his arm, feeling its strong purr thrumming against his wrist. He brought the counter close to its body and the needle jumped a little way up the scale. Griffiths raised his eyebrows.

EPICENTER

"Not high enough for a fatal dose."

He hoisted the cat more comfortably under his arm and followed Anders through the revolving door.

The two men had volunteered to be dropped near the lower end of downtown to monitor the radiation level at key locations indicated on a street map. Their sector to inspect had escaped the brunt of the fire, and most of the buildings were untouched. Other two-man teams had been dropped by helicopter at strategic points and were fanning out in accordance with a master plan to monitor the whole city. The fire had burned out completely, but it was still physically too hot for teams to check inside the destroyed area, and there was also the danger of collapsing buildings. The teams had strict instructions to radio for helicopters to take them out of any danger area immediately, and they could call on the helicopters to act as aerial taxis if needed.

The flow of contaminated air from Fairfield station had been stopped. The last bolt had been driven on the dome and the steel tow ropes secured ready to pull it away. Now Waring wanted to be sure that the contamination level in the city was safe before allowing people to return.

The carpet in the hotel foyer was crumpled and muddy. Armchairs had been overturned. The chandeliers were still on, and Griffiths instinctively looked to the wall to find a switch to turn them off. On the other side of the registration desk the cash-register drawer had been wrenched out; the drawer was empty. A woman's silk scarf lay on the counter, and nearby a man's empty billfold. Across the foyer were the remains of a large mirror smashed into a thousand fragments.

They walked through the tomblike hall silently, the only sound the crunching of their suits. Anders took a note pad from his breast pocket. He read the level on the monitor and jotted down the figure. They hesitated outside the row of elevators. The green Up lights glowed brightly in the subdued light, and the elevator doors were open. The same thought crossed their minds: wonder if anybody's upstairs?

"You stay outside and I'll see if the doors close when I'm inside. If they won't open again you can prize them open." Griffiths nodded. Anders entered the elevator and hesitated before finding the right button. The doors came together smoothly. He pressed another button and they slid open.

"Going up!" he called. Griffiths laughed and stepped inside.

"Seems okay here," Anders said, pointing to the monitoring instrument. "We'd better check upstairs." He pressed a button at random. The doors slid silently together and the elevator moved upward. The sign inside announced: Visit the Star Spangled Room. Hear the Scintillating Music of Rodger Ricky at the Keyboard. Open Now for Your Relaxing Pleasure. A broken turned-inside-out umbrella lay in the corner of the elevator and, curiously, a torn black nightie that must have fallen from a woman's suitcase.

The elevator stopped and the doors opened. Griffiths stepped out behind Anders. They glanced at the monitors and Anders recorded a figure. There was no sign of contamination —the massive outside structure of the hotel had acted as a shield. Anders went to the window in the elevator hallway and tested the instrument again. The needle on the gauge jumped upward slightly, but steadied well within the safe limit.

"Pretty good. Wonder what the reading was last week?" he asked. Griffiths shrugged his shoulders.

"Let's see what it reads at the east end of the building, facing Fairfield," Anders suggested. He strode around the corner and collided with an abandoned dinner trolley. The tureens still stood on the top shelf. Griffiths lifted a cover; inside were crinkled baked potatoes turning black. In the other were clumps of rotting cauliflower. He wrinkled his nose and laughed.

"Dinner for two?" Anders asked gruffly. He pushed the trolley to the wall.

They walked noiselessly along the carpeted corridor past open bedroom doors, and went inside several of the rooms. The beds were unmade. A pair of brown shoes lay inside the door in one room where the owner had overlooked them in his haste to leave. Personal belongings were strewn across the dressing table in another, and a walking stick and a parcel of laundry lay on the bed in another room. Halfway along the corridor a linen trolley had been overturned, the fresh bed-clothes torn and footmarked where people had walked on them. Anders stopped to take a reading.

Griffiths shuddered as he waited. It was eerie and unreal. Suddenly music blasted from the far end of the corridor. They looked up in disbelief.

"Someone must have left the radio on!" Griffiths yelled, but the music was so loud that Anders could not hear him. It couldn't be a local station broadcasting that stuff, Anders thought, listening to the raucous noise. They're operating under the general emergency.

Their hoods muffled the sound, but as they approached they could hear people laughing and shouting. The noise came from an open door at the end of the corridor. Anders pointed to an ornate sign on the wall: York Suite. He hunched his shoulders.

At the door both men stared at the colored crayoned sign —End of the World Party. Under the high chandeliers hung New Year's Eve tinsel and ribbons, and gay party balloons floated near the ceiling. The furniture had been pushed to the side of the room, and there was a bar with bottles, glasses, and food. The racket came from a record player, and half-naked couples were dancing wildly to the thumpings of the deafening dissonance. There were about fifty men and women tightly packed in the middle of the floor, their bodies swinging separately or together. One lanky man pulsated around the floor locked in embrace with a naked curvaceous blonde whose eyes were tightly closed, her face strained in a paroxysm of pleasure as her clinging body swung forward and backward in rhythm to the man's movements.

Griffiths wanted to tear his eyes away to look at Anders, but the living orgy held him. Anders reacted first. He tiptoed away—an unnecessary precaution—and raced along the corridor to the elevator hallway. Griffiths ran after him. Anders switched on the radio but the equipment was useless inside the building. They stepped into the elevator and Griffiths pressed the button.

In the middle of the street Anders contacted EMO headquarters. There was nothing they could do about the party until Anders reported the downtown area safe to re-enter. They walked up University Avenue, the thoroughfare that caused the collective bosom of Toronto's City Council to swell with civic pride. It was their show street: a boulevard of adjoining lawns in the center, green in summer, fringed with concrete boxes of flowers that made the street a burst of color. Now the boulevard lay under snow, framed by the sterile concrete-and-glass office buildings on either side. The sun was still high and the shadows and sunlight played tricks with the eye, making the deserted avenue sparkle innocently with reflected light. Three smashed cars were at the next intersection, their windshields shattered and their front wheels buckled.

Griffiths looked inside one car. The stiff corpse of a smartly dressed woman was jammed behind the wheel, her daintily gloved hands clutching the broken rim. Her face was as white as the snow that had driven through the partly opened window and covered the front seat.

"Must have been here since evacuation night," Anders said grimly. He spoke into the radio and made a note in his book. He looked up the broad avenue. The snow lay undisturbed in both north- and southbound lanes. Except for the wrecks, there was not another vehicle in view. They continued northward, passing the empty Canadian Press building. The three big metropolitan daily newspapers had evacuated the city and were attempting to publish from Barrie and Orillia, using the printing facilities of the local newspapers.

At the Court House Anders stopped and checked the radioactivity. It had dropped.

"It's practically nothing here, Joe. I think we can take off the visors."

"It always steams up on me," Griffiths replied, swiveling the transparent shield from his face.

They were outside the General Hospital, an old building on College Street that sat smugly behind a high iron fence. Like the Children's Hospital and the Mount Sinai Hospital nearby, the General had been evacuated. Critically ill patients had been loaded into the few available ambulances and taxis, but most of them had simply been loaded into buses which then became stalled in the dense traffic jams. Stiff corpses arrived at the portable hospitals set up in the evacuation centers.

They cut through to Yonge Street. The neon signs still flashed on and off in the afternoon sun. The wide glass windows of the big Woolworth's had been smashed and goods torn off the display stands, counters swept clean, and every cash register toppled. Anders calmly surveyed the scene. He took a reading, noted the level, and nodded to Griffiths to follow.

EPICENTER

Something drew him to the subway entrance. The lights were on over the stairs leading down, but it was dark in the station hall. It took them a few seconds to find out why. From the floor to the ceiling the space was jammed with people—dead people. Arms and legs stuck out grotesquely, and pieces of torn clothing littered the concrete floor.

"My God!" Griffiths murmured. "They must have smothered in the panic to get down. It happened in London during the blitz. We—"

"Let's get out!" Anders shouted, his face suddenly gray. "I'll call control!" On the sidewalk he spoke in a low voice to headquarters.

They walked on slowly, past stores with broken windows where remnants of looted merchandise lay untidily. The gasoline pumps of a service station at the next corner were sheared off at the ground, smashed when some vehicle rammed into them.

"Let's take another reading," Anders said roughly. "If it's low here there's no point in going further."

The monitor needle barely moved from normal. "It's even lower here," he said. "I'll call for a chopper to pick us up. It could land at this intersection—it's clear of overhead wires." Griffiths seemed uncertain. "What if the wind blows another stream of contamination father north? The land starts to rise here," he said, pointing up the street.

"You could be right, Joe. But I'd hate to have to walk all that way and find the readings are normal. Let's call the chopper and get a lift to Eglinton Avenue—that's about two miles up."

"Good idea."

The helicopter settled gently at the intersection. When they were aboard and rising the pilot grinned and yelled to Anders: "Thought you guys were walking all the way to

Aurora!" Anders smiled, but he didn't think it was funny.

The machine landed near the subway-bus station at the Yonge and Eglinton intersection and then departed. Anders looked at the monitor. It was up, close to the danger mark. He yanked the visor down on Griffiths' face and pulled his own into position.

"Straight up!" he shouted, indicating north. The silence was more unsettling here than downtown. The traffic lights at the intersections flashed from green to amber to red with ghostlike precision, signaling commands to nonexistent traffic. They walked steadily, stopping at each intersection to take readings. At the next major cross street, Anders suggested they duck down a side street. "We'll check outside the houses on the way."

The mellowed brick and stone-faced houses in the tree-lined streets off Yonge Street were pleasingly designed with lead-paned windows in front and pleasant oriel windows at the sides. The leafless elms that arched across the street softened the view and partly hid the ugly overhead electric cables.

They stopped at the corner and looked up the street. Several cars were parked at the curb about two hundred yards ahead, and a furniture moving van was backed into a driveway. Two men stepped from a house, struggling with a large dining table, which they lifted into the back of the van.

"Hey, what's up?" Griffiths shouted behind his visor.

"Looters," Anders replied. He pushed Griffiths behind a thick tree trunk. "If they see us we'll be slugged. I'll tell control. Then we can back down the street!"

Griffiths peeked from behind the tree. Two more men came out of a house not far away, one carrying a television set on his head, the other a case of golf clubs. Griffiths' face was muddy with anger.

Anders switched off. "C'mon—let's get back to Yonge Street!" he said, darting behind the trees for cover.

They stopped at the city limits where the road swept down to Hogg's Hollow to meet Highway 401 about a half mile north. It was the end of the route marked on Anders' map. The reading was nil. He flicked on the radio.

"Clean as a whistle at city limits. Normal on the monitor. How about a lift to Aurora?"

"We'll send a chopper in a few minutes. Signal to let the pilot know where's a landing spot clear of overhead wires," a precise voice said.

"Okay—out."

"That looks like a good place over there, in the parking lot," Anders said, pointing across the road. "Let's get over."

Ten minutes later a helicopter roared overhead. They waved wildly and the pilot settled the machine on the parking lot. Anders ducked his head and ran to the door held open by an EMO man. They climbed aboard. "What've you got there?" the EMO man yelled above the din in the cabin. Griffiths followed the man's staring eyes. They were riveted to a furry shape under Griffiths' arm, a black bundle that slowly unwound into two friendly yellow eyes and a red mouth that yawned in contented boredom.

FIFTEEN

The steel cables connected to the dome twanged as the tractors took up the slack. Johnson raised his hand and the vehicles
stopped. He had put on coveralls since he'd moved to Fairfield from the mobile base and now strode to where Deighton
sat in a jeep some distance from the dome.

"We'll take a count now," Johnson said, reaching into the
jeep and taking out two portable geiger counters. He shoved
one in Witzensky's hand.

The two men approached the dome, holding the counters
at waist level, heads bent as they watched the needles. They
walked in a steadily decreasing spiral until the counters
scraped against the gray-silver surface of the dome. The
needles rose slightly above normal, wavered, then steadied
inside the green lines.

"It's okay!" Johnson shouted, his voice dulled inside the
visor. "Now for the cut."

He signaled to Deighton that it was safe to start the cutting
knives under the rim of the dome. A powerful electric motor
had been bolted to the top of the dome, and heavy wires
snaked across the muddy snow to a portable switchboard con-

nected to the main power supply in the street. The jeep turned and drove over to the switchboard. Deighton jumped down.

"Everybody stand well back!" he commanded. He looked like a skinny dwarf inside the protective coveralls. His long drooping mustache seemed to drag his bony face into the body of the suit until only his alert eyes peeped out of the stiff neckpiece.

Witzensky's rescue team and the assembly men moved away. They had used up their exposure allowances. If the knives didn't work, Deighton would have to call his scientific group together again and ask for new volunteers to carry out whatever new scheme they devised.

He reached for a switch and pushed it down. The motor groaned, buzzed, and settled into a low roar. He allowed it to warm up for a full minute, then moved his hand to another lever, the lever that would throw the motor into gear and start the knives whirling. He glanced over his shoulder and his eyes met Johnson's. They peered through the visors for long seconds, and each knew what the other was thinking. They'd worked closely together in the past two weeks, long enough to appreciate each other's special knowledge and weaknesses, and they knew what was at stake. The moment ended, and Deighton shifted his gaze past Johnson to the rim of the dome where it rested on six wheels. He yanked down the lever.

The rim started to turn, increasing in speed as he put pressure on the lever. The knives built into the rim unfolded, bit into the frozen asphalt. Long strips of sodden tar lashed under the dome and were flung clear. The knives sliced through the top layer and cut into the roadbed. Bits of broken gravel shot from under the rim. The dome began to sink. The space between the rim and the ground diminished. Encouraged, Deighton applied more pressure and pushed the lever fully down. The ground vibrated. Chunks of rubble rattled inside the dome with tremendous force, ricocheting off the metal structure with the sound of sharp thunderclaps. Johnson bent down to check the gap under the dome, and a stony sliver whipped past his ear. Deighton waved for him to keep clear. The rim quickly settled into the ground. The fiercely biting knives grew quieter as they descended deeper into the earth.

Only a few more minutes and Deighton could slow the knives and turn the control to fold them under to form a floor. But the dome suddenly tilted, churning up a wave of half-frozen muck that flew into the air and splashed in a semi-circle at his feet. He slammed up the switch to cut the power. Even as the motor moaned and stopped, the dome sank four feet on its side into the excavation it had cut.

The assemblymen rushed to the ugly hole in the ground. "Get back! Get back!" Johnson yelled, waving the geiger counter.

Unused to working in a radioactive-contaminated environment, the men had instinctively run to find out what had gone wrong. They fell back, and Johnson and Witzensky cautiously approached, checking the counters. They stalked around the dome. Surprisingly, the counters pinged slowly.

"The earth and rubble are acting as a shield," Johnson explained.

"Where the hell do we go from here? We can't fold the knives back with the dome tipped like that," Deighton shouted, though the motor had died.

"Why not?" Johnson asked on sudden impulse.

Deighton's eyebrows shot up and his mustache worked in little flips. He swore inside his visor. They had calculated the weight of the structure carefully. There must be a soft spot in the earth caused by a partial thawing of the ground—it happened often during the Toronto winters where the weather was moderated by the vast lake on the city's doorstep. Deighton was an Ottawa man, where the winters were more severe and the ground was frozen solid well into March.

"We could try it—but slowly," he decided, reaching for the switch. "Everybody back!"

He pushed it down, and the motor revved up. He pulled down the lever with a deliberate, slow movement. Earth and stones drummed against the interior of the dome, and then there was a whirring sound as the knives hinged upward, grabbing the rubble and clay. He moved the lever upward and switched off. The motor whined and stopped.

"Test for radiation!" he ordered.

Johnson approached with Witzensky. The dome was a drunken man's derby that perched at an absurd angle on top of a buried head. What about the tow now? It would be impossible for the tractors to pull the dome away when it was tipped like that. He went up to Deighton.

"How'll we get the cockeyed thing away now?"

Deighton sucked cold air in through his breathing vent, shrugged his shoulders, and turned away. At least the radiation around the dome wasn't dangerous, so they could approach within two feet without being unduly exposed. That was something to be thankful for. But he knew it was impossible to tilt the structure upright with the tractors.

The other team, working in relays near the reactor building, reported that their problem was of a long-term nature. The heavy water had disappeared through the foundations of the building but odd pockets of high radiation levels still remained, with death a certain result of overexposure, despite protective suits. A rescue captain had mustered his team and sent them in in relays, keeping track of their exposure times.

One man used up his precious allowance in half the calculated safe time; he would not be allowed to work in a nuclear plant for the next six months.

Concrete footings had to be chipped away where the heavy water had left a damp coating, and firehoses had been brought in to wash down the pipes and auxiliary equipment. It would be months before Reactor Number One would be working again. Every square inch of the inside of the building would have to be painstakingly inspected, and the pressure tubes repaired.

"We should use a helicopter to lift the whole bloody thing in the air and dump it in the lake," Johnson said mechanically, his voice overlaid with irony.

Deighton swung around, his eyes suddenly alight.

"You've got it!" he shouted. "A skyhook!"

His excitement ignited Johnson's face. He turned to the small knot of engineers who had come from EMO headquarters.

"Anyone here know the lifting capacity of the helicopters —those big fellas, the ones we had at Aurora?" he demanded.

Ray Johnson looked up, squinting against the strong sunlight. His calculations had shown they would need three helicopters to lift the heavy dome, and they now hovered above the station, connected by a steel rope bridle that hung in graceful arcs. He could see the safety break-joints near the fuselage of each machine which would quickly disconnect if an uneven tug on the bridle tipped the helicopter off balance. The big hooks on the end of the steel cables that hung loosely from each machine were clanging against the steel dome. The electric power line to the dome had been disconnected and now lay in a neat coil near the switchboard.

An Armed Forces officer near the jeep spoke into a microphone, but his words were drowned out by the deafening roar reverberating between the concrete buildings. The fluff-fluff-fluff of the giant rotors was amplified in the confined space, re-echoing between the walls.

Three steel loops had been welded to the dome. At a signal from the officer, Johnson nodded to Witzensky, who approached the dome with two men carrying poles which they used to catch the suspended hooks and skillfully maneuver them through the loops. The officer's lips moved again, telling the pilots that the hooks were engaged. The rotor blades beat the air at a different angle, and the engine note changed as the pilots took up the slack in the cables. The wires vibrated wildly, and the bridle between the three helicopters throbbed with a wavelike motion. Everybody stared upward. The waves subsided, then died in little ripples against the break-joints.

Johnson looked up, carefully weighing in his mind the balance of the dome when it lifted. He'd ordered the cable from the rearmost helicopter to be made longer than the others to allow for the tilt.

The engine note again changed. The three helicopters moved apart to tighten the bridle—not too much, or the joints would break. Quickly, with no preamble, no announcement, the air was filled with an ear-splitting blast as the pilots opened the throttles simultaneously, throwing the rotors into full lift. The cables strained, then distended into three straight lines. The bottom of the dome shuddered, lurched, moved upward an inch, then suddenly emerged from the hole. Chunks of asphalt, smashed rubble, and showers of gravel fell away. Three feet, ten, twenty—the massive steel-and-lead thing soared up swiftly. It rose to the top of the reactor buildings, the roar from the engines quickly died, and the trail of loose dirt became a trickle. The officer calmly spoke into the microphone, shielding his eyes from the sun. The helicopters stopped and hovered as one unit. Johnson's eyes gleamed with admiration. The engine notes changed for the last time, and the machines moved off, each held on station by the bridle.

They moved over the reactor building, rotor blades flashing, the tilted dome with its radioactive cargo a giant turtle shell following obediently on the end of three puppet strings. It vanished behind the humped roof of the reactor buildings, the cables disappeared, and then the helicopters as the pilots set course for the burial ground prepared for the dome at Atomic Energy's research plant at Chalk River, up the Ottawa Valley.

Fairfield was clean again. Johnson rubbed his jaw and suddenly realized he was still looking up at the sky. A ragged cheer sounded from the assembly men, and several wild spirits clapped and jumped with the release of tension. One man threw his yellow hardhat in the air, and it landed in the hole where seconds earlier the dome and its contaminated load had lain half buried.

Deighton rushed to the jeep, grabbed the radio microphone, and held down the switch. "Fairfield to General Waring, EMO Headquarters, Aurora. The fuel bundles have been safely removed from Fairfield. They're on their way by aerial transportation to Chalk River as arranged!" he called breathlessly. He threw the microphone on its hook and turned to Johnson. "Thanks to your skyhook idea!"

He grasped Johnson's hand, and Johnson shook it self-consciously. The radio buzzed, and General Waring's gruff voice came through the speaker.

"Good work, Deighton. I'm ordering Operation R into effect immediately. Put Johnson on, will you? I want to congratulate him!"

SIXTEEN

Operation R was the General's plan for returning two million people to the city that he'd drawn up with Ferrisston and a group of EMO and Armed Forces logistic experts. People would be allowed back in a controlled flow, to avoid the accidents and breakdown of law and order that had occurred during the evacuation.

The news from Fairfield burst upon the scattered communities of evacuees with the power of a tidal wave, sweeping them up in a rush of enthusiasm that had one immediate reaction: everybody wanted to get home as quickly as possible. But Waring had done his planning well.

"All persons heading back to Toronto from the reception centers must wait for the EMO officials to give the signal that return is authorized . . ." the government-directed radio stations announced. "Be patient; the EMO and other government authorities will get you home as soon as possible. Special gasoline deliveries are being made to all service stations whose supplies are exhausted . . ."

"It's all over! Thank God!" Alice MacGregor sighed. "Just think. Our own beds again!" She suddenly felt tired as the

tenseness dropped away. She remembered the empty bungalow and wondered about Pam's wedding. They'd have to
make new arrangements at the church now. She hoped there
wouldn't be much delay. It was bad enough Pam having to
put off the wedding when Jock died, and then having to run
away like this.

"What did Ken say when you saw him in Orillia?" she
asked.

"We're gonna get married the first Saturday we get back
to town—even if the church's burned down!"

Alice MacGregor was stunned. "What! You know they'll
have to call the banns again and you'll have to see the vicar
about the arrangements and get the—"

"Ken said we'll have a civil ceremony if necessary, and
then—"

"You'll do no such thing!" her mother interrupted. "You'll
get married in church or—"

"Let me finish, Mother!" Pamela came into the kitchen, a
freshly ironed dress over her arm. "Afterward we'd have the
church ceremony—just as we arranged. He said—"

"He said! He said! Haven't you got a mind of your own?"

"Mother!"

"I'm sorry, Pam. I know your father wouldn't like it. Married in an office, I mean."

"But we'd get married in church later, after we come back
from our honeymoon. Don't you see, Mother? It'll be the
same thing. It might be months before we can get married if
we have to wait for the church. Besides, it might really have
been burned down." She folded the dress carefully and
packed it away.

"Well, we'll see how things are when we get home," her
mother said philosophically, as if that settled everything.

EPICENTER

"Look! The Toronto skyline!" Pamela exclaimed, pointing through the windshield. "Looks all right to me!"

They peered above the roof of the car in front as it dipped over the final rise before the land rolled away to the city by the lake. The late-afternoon sun cast a soft brilliance over the distant concrete towers that marked the sprawling metropolis not many miles away. An airplane crossed low overhead, followed by a helicopter flying north. Then a DC-9 swept in over the western sky, its high-set tail strongly silhouetted against the golden light.

"Air Canada's flying again," Andy said authoritatively. "Remember, they said on the radio all flights had been stopped 'cos of radioactivity?"

"Everything's gonna be all right," Pamela said with conviction, now that they were nearly home. "Wonder if Ken can make it today?"

"They won't let the Orillia people home till they've cleared the Barrie people first, and from the other places around about, dear," her mother said.

The drive along Highway 401 toward Fairfield took much less time than their rush in the opposite direction two weeks before. Pamela swung the car down the ramp leading to the nuclear-station neighborhood. She slowly turned into the street to the little community of bungalows with the pleasantly colored roofs. Just two more blocks and they'd be home. She rounded the corner, and the trim brick building with the snow-covered front lawn faced them.

They sat in the car in the driveway, silently looking at the windows, the roof, the tall television antenna, and then back to the front door. Alice MacGregor spoke first. "Andy, you forgot to put the snow shovel away again," she said, looking at the offending implement propped up on the porch.

"Okay, Mom! Right away!" he replied in a simulated harried voice. "Let's go—what're we waiting for?"

Inside the little hallway a familiar household smell brought a flood of recollection. Pamela and Andy rushed to their rooms. Alice opened the front closet. Jock's everyday parka and his best topcoat hung inside, the gray coat with the smart double vent in the back. She ran her hand down the sleeve, holding back the tears. It seemed an eternity since she'd stood with her children at the edge of the grave, while the clergyman intoned words whipped away by the bitterly cold wind. She'd sell the bungalow as soon as Andy finished the school year. With Pam married she wouldn't need such a big place. She and Andy could get on nicely in a small apartment. They were going to build a whole new subdivision not far away, she remembered. What was it called? Belltop Heights Estates—yes, that was it. She'd heard they were going to rent quite reasonably. She'd make inquiries. But now she'd better clean up the house. The dust was everywhere.

SEVENTEEN

"I'll drive you all the way home," Rita said firmly.

"It's awful good of you, Rita," Rosie Long said. "We'd never 'ave made it so early if we'd gone in the bus." She turned to Shirley in the back seat. "Won't be long now," she said. The girl spread her mouth in a wide grin and looked through the window. They were driving past rows of houses in the northwest district of the city. Here and there a car swung off the street and braked in a driveway, the doors burst open, and children ran out, followed by adults, who stretched themselves and looked up at the buildings.

"Come and have a cup of coffee with me at my apartment," Rita said. She dreaded the moment when she'd open the door and be left on her own. Her body stiffened, and she rebuked herself. She was losing her grip. Tomorrow she'd go to the head office and check what was doing with the new spring dresses, then see about the branch requirements.

"Wouldn't want to put you to no trouble, Rita." Rosie Long felt obligated. She was grateful for the ride back to the city.

"No trouble. It's not far from here."

EPICENTER

Nothing seemed to have changed as she stood looking up at the tall modern apartment block. The snow had melted in the Japanese garden that bordered the curved driveway, exposing the weathered stones. She smelled the damp, fresh odor of earth, and filled her lungs with the sweet fragrance. People hurried by, bustled with hand luggage, propping the doors open to let each other in. The elevator was crowded with unknown faces.

"It's the eleventh," Rita said. "Bit of a drag up." Rosie nodded. She was used to riding elevators in strange highrise apartments. Many of her customers were young marrieds without children, and she cleaned up while they were both out to work.

Strangely, there was no cooking odor as they got out. Rita fished for a key, opened the door, and threw the two flight bags on the floor. It was cold: the heat hadn't fully come on yet. She went into the bedroom and hastily gathered up the lingerie she'd strewn over the bed when she'd packed.

"Make yourselves at home," she called to Rosie and Shirley.

"Shall I put the coffee on, Rita?"

"Okay, thanks. You'll find the perk on the stove." She kicked off her shoes.

The coffee warmed them. "Say, I nearly forgot," Rita said, turning to Shirley. "Your dress. Let's measure it for the alteration." She went down to the car, brought back the dress, and held it against the girl's tall, thin form.

"Here, come and see!"

Rita stood her before the full-length mirror in the bathroom. "Ahh—ahh—Ree—tah!" Shirley gasped, and smiled happily.

"It'll be her party dress," Rosie said. "She's never had one special like," she added with meaning.

"I'll give you a call when I get in touch with the tailor,"

EPICENTER

Rita said. "It'll probably be ready next week. I'll drive you home now."

"Oh!" Rosie uttered breathlessly. They were in the midtown streets, where the smart boutiques and fashion shops drew the Saturday crowds, and had stopped before the entrance of a street blocked solid with debris. They looked down the street, at the burned hulks of what had been stores and small office buildings, where wisps of black smoke still curled upward. A policeman approached.

"You can't go down there," he said sternly. "Didn't you see the detour sign?"

"No—where was it?" Rita said.

"Back about a hundred yards. You'll have to back up and go down Yonge Street. Where you headed for, anyways?"

"Cabbagetown."

The policeman shook his head gravely. "Not much use you going there. It's nearly all burnt to the ground."

"We don't live right in Cabbagetown—a bit east," Rosie looked anxiously into the policeman's face.

"Well, you can try. A bit east, you say. Better go along Bloor and down Parliament Street. Maybe you'd avoid all this." He nodded at the rubble and blackened ruins.

"Thanks, officer."

A rope had been rigged up across Parliament Street to stop traffic. "We'll have to walk," Rita said, glancing at two policemen on the other side of the rope.

They slowly got out of the car. One of the policemen intercepted Rita as she ducked under the rope. He waved her back.

"But this lady and her daughter live down this way," she protested.

"That's right. On Cross Street," Rosie said.

EPICENTER

The officer stroked his chin. "Hey, Charlie," he called to the other. "Where's Cross Street? These people say they live there."

The policeman hesitated. He looked at the three women, then at the car. "I don't think they managed to save more'n three or four houses on Cross. What number's yours?"

"Forty-seven," Rosie replied, fear gripping her. "The one with the attic window overlooking the street. It's not like the others. They've got their attic windows at the back."

"Can't expect me to remember all the details," the officer said. "All I remember is there's a few left standing. All right, Bert, I guess it's okay to let 'em through."

Both sides of Parliament Street lay in ruins. They stepped cautiously over crashed chunks of broken masonry and smelled the acrid stink of charred wood. The variety store on the corner of Cross Street had somehow miraculously half escaped the flames. The bottom story was intact, and candies and toys in the window seemed untouched even though the front door was open. A pile of old newspapers lay inside, the edges crisped by the searing heat but the centers strangely untouched.

Rosie turned the corner and stared up Cross Street. Four or five houses stood intact about halfway along the block. Blackened electric cables and telephone wires were strewn everywhere, and bricks and crackled timbers were scattered about. They hurried on, afraid to look at the scarred front doors of the houses that still stood upright amid a scene of desolation. The odd numbers were on the south side. Rita quickly counted—forty-one, forty-three, forty-five, forty . . . Rosie's shrill scream died as Rita spun her around and buried the agonized face against her shoulder.

EPICENTER

Rita opened the apartment window despite the cool air inside. She felt confined, as though the events of the past few hours had compressed her into a hard ball. Rosie Long had refused to come back to stay with her. She could have managed somehow to put them up, at least for the night. In the end Rosie and Shirley had gone to a church hall taken over by the EMO and now serviced by the Salvation Army. There were several temporary resting places for the dispossessed set up near the burned-out area.

She poured a Scotch and sat at the dining table. It was suddenly very quiet inside the apartment. Her eyes dimmed, as though a veil had dropped behind her eyeballs. The uncertain something which had so long lain dormant deep inside and had tightened into a cold knot of suffering suddenly broke to the surface with shattering violence. Her skin went cold. Her fingers trembled as they held the glass. She lifted it to her lips but her mouth shook so convulsively that the cool liquid spilled over the polished tabletop. Her body shook uncontrollably. Then the tears came, hot tears that poured on to her arms as she dropped her head on the table.

The tumult ended as suddenly as it had begun. She went to the bathroom and washed her face in cold water. Then she undressed, showered, and wrapped herself in a robe. She sat in the armchair and picked up the handbag from the side table near the telephone, searching for a cigarette. For the first time since she'd got back to the city she could think clearly. Ray would likely have taken part in cleaning up the mess at the power station. He might even have been hurt or trapped. Hardly—he knew how to handle himself: he might even have been a hero!

No, not Ray! Too deliberate. He always had to be sure. Never took a chance. She smiled, remembering a trip in the cable car over the Whirlpool Rapids at Niagara Falls. And the look on the man's face when Ray gravely asked about the strength of the cables. She was half convinced he was pulling the man's leg, but he looked so serious.

Perhaps her own life would have been fuller if they had stuck it out. Four years wasn't that long. It might have been different if they'd had a baby. She sniffed and brushed her eyes with her fingers. A baby would have taken up her time, spoiled her figure, interfered with her career. But it would have brought them closer together. Her married friends with babies had told her that. She flicked the ash off the cigarette and noticed that her hands had stopped trembling.

It would mean a big sacrifice—too much to expect. She'd built up a reputation on The Avenue, and Morris Weinstein had come to rely on her absolutely. But what about herself? What had she got out of it? Material things, and a sense of achievement, some deep elemental feeling that gave her a sense of security, of importance.

She rested her head on the back of the armchair, eyes half closed, watching the smoke layers drift in the still room.

She leaned forward, impatiently stubbed out the cigarette, and picked up the telephone.

Ray Johnson lay on the couch he'd borrowed from Townsend and dug his head into the soft cushion. Deighton had ordered him home for a couple of days while a skeleton staff of operators made a thorough survey of the damage at the power station. "Don't worry. They'll give you a buzz if they need you," Deighton had told him, grinning. Johnson didn't argue. The tension hadn't surfaced in him as it had in the others. Their faces had become lined, and hollows had appeared under their eyes.

His reaction had set in the moment the helicopters lifted

the dome high above the station roof. He drove the short distance to his place in a daze, and made a meal from canned vegetable soup and spaghetti. The bread was brick-hard. Tomorrow he'd go shopping at the supermarket, if it was open. He hadn't thought about that. It might be days before they brought in fresh food. But that was tomorrow. Now was the time to relax, to rest. A heavy weight dropped from him. He wondered what the designers of Fairfield would do to prevent a repetition of the million-to-one chance of a severe earth tremor occurring at the same time as fuel bundles were being changed. He'd heard of a California engineer's idea to build nuclear stations on man-made floating islands off the coast. If an earthquake struck the whole island would simply ride it out, with its power plant unaffected.

He dozed off as the warmth of the hot bath he'd taken permeated his body. When he awoke the room was in semi-darkness. The sun had set, and a cool breeze stirred outside the open window. A feeling of well-being enveloped him. Rita would be on her way home now. She'd probably already be telephoning her business friends, arranging appointments. Whatever happened, whatever catastrophe struck, she'd act as if it were business as usual. Nothing must interfere with the money-making, the deals, the advantage-seeking.

Maybe it was better this way, the separation. But they'd had some good times together. When she forgot those damned women's dresses and coats she was real fun. A smile played around his mouth. They'd gone fishing with another couple in a rented boat. Rita had caught the only fish, and even though they'd changed positions in the boat she still was the only one to pull them in. And the impromptu dance and sing-song they'd had at the cabin later, when the two other couples joined them. Lucky thing that fellow from Texas had had a portable record player and Rita had remembered the drinks.

EPICENTER

He yawned and scratched the top of his head. He was thinking how much effort it would be to get up and walk the few steps to the refrigerator to see if there was any beer left, when the telephone rang.